GREAT WHITE THRONE

From his presence earth and sky fled away

GREAT WHITE THRONE

Ω

J.B. SIMMONS

Book Three of the Omega Trilogy

www.jbsimmons.com
jbsimmons.light@gmail.com
@jbsimmonslight

Cover by Kerry Ellis
www.kerry-ellis.com

ISBN 1514302136

For the only perfect man,
the one who teaches
how to live in the present
with an eye to eternity

Ω

My name is Elijah Goldsmith. This is my story, and it's the honest-to-god truth. I heard Him. I believe now. But that doesn't make it any easier, because I still can't see the ending. Oh, you and I know what people say about the ending, but no one really knows. No one can predict the last day. No one can tell me what's going to happen to Naomi and the baby. My visions grow stronger, though. And the things I see fill me with fear wrapped thick around a tiny core of hope. What will remain if everything burns?

1

I STOOD BEFORE a man on a throne. I couldn't see his face or much of anything else, because something bright blazed before me. I felt like I was staring at a supernova.

I tried turning away, but as I spun, the man and the light stayed fixed in front of me. I twisted to the left, then to the right. I stepped backwards. None of it helped. The man, the throne, and the light were squarely before me no matter where I looked, no matter how fast I turned. Everything on the fringes of my vision was pure white.

I tried closing my eyes, pressing my hands over them. The light still blazed into me. There was no escape.

I stopped resisting. I let the light wash over me like a warm shower.

I stepped toward it.

One foot.

Then the next. Brighter. Warmer.

With each step through the vastness, the light burned less. Moving closer to the source of the light made it seem farther away.

I could see the throne and the man better now. The throne was pearly smooth. Its surface faded into the sea of white around me. The man might have had a beard. He might have worn a robe and a crown. I forgot about all those things when our eyes connected. "Eyes" wasn't quite right. They were where a person's eyes would be on a face, but they were like universes of galaxies and stars concentrated into marble spheres.

I realized I'd stopped walking. I couldn't bring myself to take another step. Now that I could see those eyes, I felt exposed. I felt guilty.

I also felt fear. Deep, paralyzing fear.

"Elijah," said another man, stepping in front of me. He blocked the universe eyes from seeing me. "We've been waiting for you."

His words made me gasp, like a burning man doused in cold water.

The man clasped my shoulder. He smiled. The whiteness around me rippled. The man's face faded.

"Elijah." Someone was shaking me, waking me. Someone with wings. Michael.

I sprang to my feet, feeling excitement and residual wonder. The two of us were in a little cave-like room in the order's hideout. Michael had sent Naomi and me to get some rest after the others in the order fled. He'd told us we had to remain until reinforcements came. He'd prayed over us, and sleep had come easily. "What time is it? Where's Naomi?"

"It's after dawn," Michael said. "She's having breakfast in the main room." He paused, studying me. "What did you dream?"

I stretched my arms and yawned. Something about the angel—an odd uncertainty—made me hesitate. "What happened to the rest of the order?"

"Gone. Ronaldo was the last to leave—a few hours ago."

"Oh." That wasn't like the Brazilian.

"He was needed elsewhere."

"So it's just the three of us . . . with Naomi ready to have her baby any time."

Michael's face was blank, statuesque.

"Shouldn't we be leaving?" I asked. "You said Don would know where we are."

"He does. We leave soon."

He'd said something similar the night before, as the order had left. He didn't give away much. I tried to convince myself that I wasn't intimidated by his black eyes with blazing fire in their centers. I pressed him, like an ant pressing a giant. "But why are we still here?"

"You'll understand in time."

"Great. Thanks." I tried to think of some way to pry. Naomi was better at this. "Can't you give me at least a *little* more than that?"

"I tell you the words I am given to tell you." The intensity of his stare made me look away. "Come, Naomi is waiting," he said. "Tell me about the dream as we walk."

He led me out of the room and we headed up a long, dimly lit tunnel. As we passed doors open to abandoned rooms, I told Michael about the throne and the universe eyes and the man who had stepped in front of the light. He nodded along. "When did this happen?"

"I don't know. There didn't seem to be time . . . if that makes sense. It seemed far away."

"It won't be for long." He sighed. "It's the gateway between this world and the one to come."

"Gateway?"

"The throne of judgment."

"As in, some people make it past, and others don't?"

"Yes."

"Then what?" The feelings of guilt and fear gripped me again, as if I were back in the dream.

"That's not my decision. My task is to get people like you to that place."

"But what happens if we don't make it through?" I couldn't shake the vision of those eyes like a universe, judging me. Suddenly nothing else seemed important. "I think I'd rather die now than get turned away."

"Dying won't save you."

"What will?"

"The man who stood between you and God's wrath."

I trembled at the way he said *wrath*. Or maybe it was just a cold draft in the hall. I swallowed, hard. "Was the

4

man Jesus?"

"I suspect it was."

"Don't you know?"

He stopped and turned to me. Something like sympathy crossed his face. "I know much of your dreams, but not all."

"If it was him, will he protect me from that . . . wrath?"

The angel studied me. "Only God knows that. It will be revealed."

"That's not much help right now. What am I supposed to do?"

"Do exactly what he told you. He said he chose you?"

I nodded, remembering Jesus's words from the day before, touching my mind in the little cave. One of his instructions still puzzled me. *Let your enemies give you quarter. In the moment when the world listens, tell the world I am coming.* I met Michael's gaze and repeated the words. Saying them filled me with energy, but also uncertainty. "I'm not sure what it means."

"You will in time. Be ready to obey. He chooses all humans for some purpose. Some refuse him, and he lets them go. You should follow what is written: *be all the more eager to make your calling and election sure.*"

"How?"

"Let's start with a good breakfast." He walked ahead, the light of his wings brushing against me. I reached out for them, but my hand passed through. He glanced back with an amused look. "Come on. Naomi is waiting."

2

MICHAEL AND I met Naomi in the hideaway's main room. It felt empty without the rest of the order. Our voices echoed off the metallic floor and walls as we ate lukewarm oatmeal. Naomi couldn't keep her eyes off Michael. He didn't say much, but we talked about the order—where they were going, where they were hiding.

Naomi seemed to know as much as he did. Probably because she'd been hidden away in this place for months. As much as she smiled and talked, something about her seemed distant. She was barely touching her food.

I pointed at her bowl. "Are you going to finish that?"

"It's all yours." She pushed it toward me. Her normally bright face was pale.

"Thanks. Are you sure you're okay?"

She put her hands over her swollen belly and faced Michael. "How much longer do we have to stay here? I feel like we're exposed."

"We are." His eyes scanned around. "No place is safe. We stay until support comes. Then we flee to the wilderness, come what may."

"You don't sound happy about it," I said.

"I obey the Lord's will." He stood from the table. His perfect form, his beautiful face—they wore an almost sad look.

Naomi leaned forward. "What's wrong?"

His hand tensed around the sword at his side. "Ages of pain and suffering and loss are coming to an end. The enemy won't go down easily. He will win battles along the way. We face trials and tribulations . . . and defeats."

"But we're going to win." Naomi's voice rose. "Even in setbacks, even in prisons and deaths, the gospel will advance. Shouldn't we be hopeful?"

Michael turned back to us. "Did the Lord hope to be crucified?"

Neither of us answered.

"Measure your hope with resolve and faith." He spread his arms wide, tilting his face toward the ceiling. His wings began to unfurl behind his back like sheets of light billowing in the wind. "No victory comes without pain. But it will be worth it." My breath froze as his wings kept unfurling, growing larger and larger until they reached the width of the enormous room. Then they snapped closed, making me gasp.

"What?" Naomi asked me.

I pointed behind Michael.

"Wings?"

I nodded.

Her eyes turned to the angel. "Why can't I see you as you are?"

"Only Elijah can see the spirit."

Spirit. Roeh. My name. I accepted now that I'd been called to this, but I still didn't understand why. "What do you mean *the spirit?*"

"The realm only you can see glimpses of." He held out his hands, studying them. "The Maker did not give my kind flesh. I was not created with this body. I have it for a limited purpose here."

"Stopping Don?" Naomi asked.

Michael's expression turned grave. "Not yet."

"If you've been an angel all this time," she pressed, "why didn't you stop Vicente before?"

Vicente—the demon Michael had killed. I looked to the spot behind me. Something like an oil stain covered the concrete floor, but the body was gone.

"He was a master of deception," Michael said. "He was far from my equal, but even lesser beings can win little victories for a time. He clouded my vision." The angel turned to me with a storm in his eyes. "The enemy let his guard down against you, and so he was revealed."

"What do you mean?" I asked, trying to hold his stare.

"Humans aren't the only ones created with different gifts," he said. "You're a seer. This demon was a liar. Lies are personal, tailored to each person's perception. The dark one didn't take you seriously enough."

"You're telling us some demon tricked you?" Naomi asked.

"Yes."

Naomi's mouth fell open in disbelief. "Could this happen again?"

"It would not be a battle if each side did not have advantages. If I knew all the enemy's movements—" His shoulders rolled back, as if flexing his muscles and wings. "Then it would be a massacre."

"But God knows everything," Naomi said.

"And how much does he tell you?" Michael challenged.

"He tells me some things. He spoke to Elijah, too." She glanced at me, then back at the angel. "You're from heaven, so shouldn't—"

"No," the angel said. "We know what is revealed to us, just as you do. Only He is unlimited by time. We were created under its dominion, like you. I know little of what's to come."

"I read about you." I remembered the words. "You and the angels, you fought against the dragon and won. You threw it down to the earth, right?"

"That was long ago. We won the war in heaven. This time it's different."

"Why?"

"Because this battle is on earth."

We were quiet for a moment, then Naomi spoke. "I've read that the dragon pursued the woman clothed with the sun, the woman who had given birth to a male child."

"Yes?"

"Is that me?"

The angel shook his head. "You are her offspring, the descendants the dragon has been at war against for over two thousand years. He has won many victories."

The somber tone in Michael's voice, however slight, was unnerving. "But you're here now," I said. "The order will rally behind you."

Michael's eyes burned into me. "You underestimate how much ground the enemy has gained. Year after year he has marched against you humans, yet you've barely noticed his advances. If you had only looked around, you would've seen he was herding you toward a cliff. Most have already fallen. Even the faithful have their heels hanging off the edge."

"But why?" Naomi asked. A wince of pain flashed across her face, her hands went to her stomach. "Why would God let this happen?"

I was surprised she'd asked the question, instead of me. Mostly, I was worried about that wince.

"It's not that simple," Michael said. "Even two thousand years is a tiny sliver of time. It amounts to nothing compared to eternity. We don't have His perspective. What matters is that He *will* win, and He *will* save those He called."

"If we know the ending," I said, "why fight?"

"We fight because we can, because it is our share of His work: to proclaim liberty to the captives, to restore sight to the blind, to—" Michael's head snapped to the side, as if he heard something. "My brothers have come. Gather your things. It's time to go."

3

NAOMI AND I went back to the little room where we'd slept. It was a dark and quiet cave with the porthole window sealed tight. I felt tempted to wrap my arms around Naomi and just hold her. If angels were coming to fight the demons, what could we do? Why not hide here until the end came?

But my eyes wandered to her large belly. No, I didn't want to be here alone when the baby came. I picked up my backpack of basic supplies—food, water, a change of clothes. "Should we bring anything else?"

"I wouldn't mind having a doctor," she said.

I laughed, shaking my head. "We'll have Michael."

"I don't feel good about this. He knows something bad is going to happen."

"Yeah, the last battle."

"Not that," she said. "He didn't sound like he was gearing up to win a fight. He sounded like he expected to lose."

"He'll take care of us. Besides, the end is coming soon."

She paused and stared at me. "Wouldn't you have seen that?"

I shook my head. "My visions never come with timelines."

"But it's not—" She grimaced, and her hands went to her stomach again.

"You okay?"

"I'm fine. Early contractions, that's all."

"How much longer do we have?"

"I wish I knew. However long, I think this baby will be born before the end."

"Why?"

"God has a plan for him."

"For an infant?"

"Yes." She sounded certain. "We know what Don thinks about the baby. He must be wrong in some way. Maybe that's why Michael wants to flee with us instead of fighting here."

"I don't know. He's the one who battled the dragon. He's the one who leads the armies. Don't you think he'll be in the middle of the fight?"

"Maybe, but only when the time is right." The sound of a rushing wind blew against the closed window, like a storm battering the rocky hillside. Naomi eyed the window. "What was that?"

"A storm?" I stepped forward and slid open the metal porthole. Naomi came to my side. Our heads touched as we peeked out at the barren terrain under a cloudless sky.

"Nothing." Naomi turned to me. "Right?"

But she was wrong. A ring of light wrapped around the hideout. It grew brighter and brighter. My breath froze as shapes started to take form.

"What is it?" she asked.

"Angels, I think." I pointed out, showing where. "They're standing shoulder to shoulder, facing out and wielding swords. They're like Michael, with wings of light behind them. No one else is in sight. Nothing dark, no enemy."

"How many?"

I started to count but quickly gave up. "I can see maybe thirty, forty from here. But there must be hundreds. They look like they're circling this place, guarding it."

I turned back to Naomi. She gaped at me in wonder.

"I want to see them!" She leaned forward to look out again. Her body was close to mine. I could feel her energy. I could smell her hair—warm, fresh, like a meadow of wild flowers.

She quickly stepped back, shaking her head. "Nothing but rocks."

"This is different," I said, still in some disbelief. "I wonder if they've been with us before. Maybe, when Jesus spoke to me, he opened my eyes to them. Maybe before that I could see only the dark spirit, and now I see both. That would explain why I now see Michael as he really is . . . and the demon."

"You're amazing."

I laughed. "You know it's not me." I gazed out the window again. This felt like the safest place on earth with the angels around us. "I still don't understand why we can't stay here."

"Because it's time to go," answered Michael's voice, a moment before he appeared in the doorway. He crossed his arms over his chest, revealing the skin under his loose sleeves. The muscles of his forearms looked like sculpted marble.

"But the angels—"

Michael raised his hand to stop me. "When the Lord returns in body, you'll know it. Until then, nowhere is safe. My brothers have their own purpose here, and we have ours. Lucifer knows where we are."

"You mean Don?" I asked.

Michael nodded. "He's coming. I have no choice."

"What does that mean?" Naomi asked. "Where are we going?"

"I told you, the wilderness. We go east."

"I don't get it," I said. "Weren't we waiting for these angels? Why leave now?"

The angel's hard gaze made me shrink back. "A time to keep," he said, "and a time to cast away."

"What's that supposed to mean?"

"It's Ecclesiastes." Naomi's eyes studied Michael. "Are

you saying we're being cast away? And why east? The Mahdi controls that area."

"We won't make it that far." Michael's gaze snapped to the window, his eyes tense. He took four quick strides and looked out. He turned to us and pointed to the door. "Step outside. Now."

We did as he said.

An instant later, I heard a huge crash. Then again, and again, like a jackhammer striking rock.

Naomi groaned lightly between two of the pounding sounds. Her face was pale again, worried.

The hammering stopped. "Come!" Michael shouted.

"Ready?" I asked Naomi.

She nodded. Her lips pressed together as if hiding something. Her eyes opened wider in surprise as she stepped into the room.

Michael was covered in dust. No tool was in sight. Light was streaming in through a man-sized hole in the cave wall. Beyond, an ocean of black shapes surged up the hillside, toward the line of defending angels.

The angel flexed his wings behind him and held his arms to us. "I will carry you."

Naomi took his hand. "I thought you could pass through walls."

"Yes, but you can't." He motioned for me to come.

"What's happening out there?" I asked.

"A legion of Lucifer has come. We must fly now."

Seeing his wings of light, listening to an angel, believing in God—those were one thing. But flying? I stepped forward uncertainly, but as soon as I did, he grabbed me and curled me under his arm like I was a sack of potatoes.

Then he charged at the hole in the wall. And jumped.

We sprang out into midair. For an instant we fell like a rock. But then we lifted and my stomach dropped as we soared up.

I glanced down in exhilarated terror at the battle erupting beneath us. The angels were like a wall of light around the hill's perimeter. The waves of black forms slammed against that wall, cracking it and pressing it back. A few racing figures had broken through the angels before I lost sight of the fighting.

As we soared ahead, Michael was staying low, rising and falling along the contours of the hilly desert terrain.

I glanced at Naomi, cradled in Michael's arms. Her hair blew back and her face glowed like the morning sun. She half-smiled, half-winced at me, and I tried to smile back. The effort allowed a little joy to seep into me from the wonder of it all. We were flying.

The angel's wings were outstretched, but not like a bird's, not like a plane's. I'd never seen anything like it. The wings were like wheels of light around us. They spun so fast that the lines blurred. I imagined, if I'd been looking up at us, I would've seen something like a glowing, soaring orb of light, with Michael holding Naomi and me in the center. His body was rigid and tense, but unmoving. Since Naomi couldn't see the wings, she must have thought Michael looked like a flying superman.

I twisted my head to look up at his face. I don't know

what I expected, maybe excitement or determination, but instead he looked uncertain, and maybe even afraid. We began flying even faster and farther from the ground. My eyes watered as the wind stung. We arced straight up into the sky, leaving the earth below. Higher and higher, colder and colder.

Then I saw something. A dark fleck in the sky.

One moment it was on the distant horizon, the next it was on top of us. It slammed into Michael. His grip around me released.

I fell. Naomi fell. We plummeted together, the wind racing past us, out of control.

Then Michael grabbed Naomi again. Then me. We spiraled down, but so did the darkness. It seemed to clamp over the angel's wings. The blurring light jerked and sputtered, ensnared in dark threads.

The ground rushed up at us. We had no wings, no parachutes.

But just as we were about to crash, Michael twisted his body sharply. A wing of light broke through the darkness, making us spin and leveling us with the ground. The angel's back hit the earth like a meteor. The sound was crushing, but his body seemed to absorb the blow. We slid to a stop.

I stood, wiggling my fingers and toes in shock. I had nothing but a few scratches. No pain. Naomi was kneeling beside me.

"Stay behind me," Michael said, staggering to his feet.

Naomi tried to rise, but stopped, putting her hands over her enlarged stomach. A tremor coursed through her body. "It barely hurt," she breathed out. "But—" she doubled over, cringing. "What *was* that?"

Michael's face went blank. A shadow passed over it. The shadow stood over us. I looked up.

The shadow was Don.

4

DON STEPPED TO Michael's side, looming over him. Shadowy threads danced around his body, as they had when I'd seen him in Scotland. When he'd killed Patrick. It was hard to believe that was just days ago.

"Show yourself," Michael demanded.

"As you wish." The shadows drifted away from Don like a morning mist over the sea, and there he stood. Black suit, red shirt. Polished, charming, and evil.

He bowed gracefully toward Naomi. "I'm delighted to see you." His voice was sharp and sophisticated. "I've been most worried about you, though Elijah's dreams gave me some comfort. How is our child?"

Naomi clutched her round belly. "He's not yours."

Don moved in a blur and was right in front of her. He

touched her cheek. "So innocent, so like Mary."

"Do not touch her." Michael slid in front of Naomi and leveled his blade at Don's throat.

"Really, a sword?" Don scoffed, but he backed away.

As they faced off, I took Naomi into my arms. Her body was trembling. So was mine. We didn't speak, didn't move. We watched in awe.

Don began to circle around the angel. "You should have learned by now, brother. You'll never be the highest angel. Does that still bother you?"

"Your words have no power over me." Michael spun as Don circled, keeping his sword between them. "We were all created to serve the King."

"That was always your problem." The smile never left Don's face. "You accept the reality as *he* made it. So unimaginative, so lacking in inspiration."

"His reality is the only reality," Michael replied, solid and smooth as steel.

"Maybe for you." Don glanced to Naomi and me. "But not for these humans. I knew it from the start. He made them to create their own reality. It took many generations, but with my help, they've made it. I will lead the final leap away from their maker."

Michael shook his head gravely. "You lead only the fallen."

"Fallen and raised, damned and saved—must you always think in black and white?" Don motioned to the surroundings. We were in a barren riverbed with no sign of life. A single dead tree stood to our left. The midday sky was immense and blue. "It is fitting that it should end here, where it began."

"What you set in motion in the garden has brought only ruin," Michael said with disdain. "You remember this place as it was. Look at it now. Another piece of creation destroyed. But that is past, Lucifer. You have already been defeated."

"You mean by his son?" Don mocked. "Your kind can keep your savior in heaven. You know he visited me. I sent him back. He didn't have the guts to reign here. But my son will." Don pointed to Naomi. "I have perfected the maker's flawed design. I rule this world. This is my story, and your kind has no part in it."

Michael's back straightened. The slight curve of a smile touched his lips. "That is your fatal flaw. It always was. You are blind to the truth: there is no reality without God. He has defeated you. We will defeat you again."

"You threaten me? *You*, here alone?" Don raised his arms and began to laugh as the shadows returned. They shrouded his body and grew into an expanding cloud of darkness.

The cloud charged at Michael, who raised his sword in a blur of light. The sound of their collision crashed like thunder.

Naomi and I cowered back, huddling close. Their movements were impossible to follow. It was like a lightning storm—the flashes revealing outlines of bodies.

Naomi groaned beside me. "It hurts, Elijah."

"The baby?" I asked, and she nodded. "They're

fighting. It's all a blur."

"Pray," Naomi whispered faintly, closing her eyes, as the thunder raged on.

I closed my eyes, too. *Pray.* I fumbled for words. *God. Help. Protect us! Please!*

Everything went quiet. Dead silence.

I opened my eyes. Don was there. Only Don.

His calm eyes and coifed hair were polished onyx. His black suit showed no blemish, as if there'd been no fight at all.

"Michael was always jealous," he said, holding out his hand to me. "You are safe now. I will take care of you and Naomi. I will give you quarter."

I shook my head, stunned. I thought of the Lord's words, as he'd spoken to me in the hideaway before the order fled. He'd told me to let the enemy give me *quarter*. And it's not like I had much of a choice. If Don had defeated Michael, I had no chance against him on my own.

Don was studying me. "Would you have her die here? You know you can't deliver a baby in the desert, alone."

"I—" *No.*

Naomi groaned.

Don took her hand, gently. "She's in labor."

Naomi did not deny it.

"I promise to protect her." Don's eyes met mine, his smile inviting. "And I do enjoy you, Elijah Goldsmith." Before, that upward curve of his lips had tugged at something inside me, almost making me want to believe him. Now I saw through it. Don swept his arms around, motioning to the empty desert. "If you have any doubt, let the archangel's fate convince you."

I held my tongue. Had Michael survived? Could an angel die?

"Where are you going to take us?" Naomi's voice was faint.

"To my new palace. It overlooks the Dead Sea, not far from Jerusalem." Don gazed to the west. "Our ride is coming."

I heard the distant sound of a plane approaching. It came into view a moment later, and with a whipping wind of sand the round disc shape touched down in front of us.

A ramp dropped open on the bottom and four androids rushed out. They moved almost like humans, but on four legs. Their gleaming metal masks had dark glass sensors for eyes. "All's ready, President," one of them said.

"Good." Don escorted Naomi forward. An android lifted her gently with its four arms and carried her up the ramp, surrounded by the other machines. I followed after them into the plane, clinging to the instructions God had given me. *Fear not our enemies. Let them give you quarter.* Maybe I was supposed to pretend Don's words and smiles still held sway over me, until the moment when the world listened.

We lifted off and flew back in the direction the plane had come. It was not long before we landed on a cliff top overlooking a bright aquamarine sea. An immense, square palace was perched on the spot. Thousands of robots were scurrying over it, as if still building. A thin glass spire rose in the center, at least as high as Don's skyscraper in Geneva. Cranes perched along the spire's sides, near the top, where a round structure sat at the pinnacle like an eagle's nest. It looked like a watchtower for the world.

"This is Masada," Don announced. "I've always been fond of the spot. Herod had a fortress here. A thousand of God's people killed themselves here. And you can't beat the view." Naomi grimaced, drawing Don's attention. "The palace will be finished soon, my woman clothed with the sun. Come, you'll like what you see."

He led us inside the palace, a train of metal with a laboring Naomi at its center. We entered a vast entry hall with black marble floors. A man in a white coat, a doctor by the looks of him, and a dozen more androids waited for us. The doctor's bony frame made him seem fragile. Large brown eyes protruded from his tense face.

"My Lord," he greeted, bowing to the floor.

"Rise," Don said. "You may take her now."

The man rose and shuffled to the robot holding Naomi and placed his skinny hand on her forehead.

"She's hot." He sounded concerned.

"She's giving birth to my son," Don said, as if that explained everything. "Now do your job. No drugs as long as you can keep the baby alive."

"Yes, my Lord." The doctor motioned for the robot to follow and turned to walk away.

"Elijah!" Naomi cried out, in obvious pain.

I moved to follow. "Wait!"

But Don's hand was on my shoulder. It froze my feet

in place.

"Let me stay with her," I pleaded.

His only answer was an amused smile. The doctor, the robot, and Naomi disappeared through a door.

5

I FELT HELPLESS as Don led me away from Naomi. She was on her own, in pain. "Don't you want to be there when your son is born?" I asked.

"No." Don kept his eyes ahead and didn't slow.

"But it's your child."

"Not completely, not yet. He has some of my enhancements. He will be ready to receive my spirit. Until I give him that, others can handle the birth."

I shook my head, failing to understand. "If the boy matters so much to you, how could you miss this? At least let me join them. Naomi needs me."

"You overestimate your importance."

Robots lined the walls beside us like sentries. Knowing, watching lights blinked in their eyes. Once or twice, I thought I glimpsed swirls of black forms sweeping past, like steam rising off the metallic creatures. There was nowhere to run. I started to break out in a clammy sweat.

"Metal and spirit." Don eyed the line of machines to his left. "These are my finest creations." He turned and motioned to my body with a look of contempt. "I never liked these human forms. Why would I care to watch one of their disgusting entrances on earth? Puny and wrinkled. Haven't you ever wondered why my enemy made you start so weak?"

I didn't have a good answer. I wiped beads of sweat from my forehead. We turned a corner. More robots, more shadows.

"Oh, bodies are capable of great fun," Don continued. "I love meddling with their desires and pains, their chemicals and libidos. But otherwise this flesh is too . . . too animal. He afflicted you poor creatures with such a flawed container."

"We can't exist without our bodies."

"Ha!" Don laughed. "You of all people know better. Maybe you can't exist without a body on this earth, but your soul still exists when the body dies. I'm offering humanity something my enemy never would, if he even could. He would make your soul subject to him. I'll allow *you* to control your soul's eternity."

His words didn't make sense, but were terrifying all the same. At least he was talking, maybe revealing hints. I tried for more. "Aren't we always subject to something? What about our bodies' needs?"

"Not in Babylon. There your desires have free reign, and they pass to your clone when your current body dies."

"I don't have a clone."

"So you think." Don smiled, keeping up his steady pace. "We'll let the androids do the work of keeping bodies alive. I'll put an end to the enemy's business of new souls. My son will be the last human born on earth."

My jaw clenched. *He's a cold-blooded killer.*

Don stopped in front of a door. He held his arms out wide and shrugged. "What's the point of your life? My enemy wants to control your purpose. I'll free you to have whatever you want."

It had to be a lie. I breathed in, out, seeking calm. "But only in a world you created."

"Exactly!" He draped his arm over my shoulder. "My world and our world, Eli." He turned with me to face the door, which slid open soundlessly. He pressed his hand to my back and urged me forward. "Go ahead, see what I offer."

I stepped inside and lost my breath. The room was like my own room in New York, only better. It had the same layout. My blanket and sheets were on the bed. The shelves held my trophies and other trinkets that were one of a kind. He'd moved my entire home.

"You took all this?" I stammered.

"I give you what you want. I hope you don't mind the changes."

The ceilings were twice as high as those in New York, and four massive chandeliers of crystal and gold dipped low and bathed the room in golden light. The floors were a rich ancient wood. The windows must have been twenty feet high, on two sides of the room.

I rubbed my temples, as if trying to confirm this was real, that I wasn't somehow in Babylon.

"How?" I asked.

"Mr. Cristo visited one week ago," said a familiar voice behind me. I turned, my mouth falling open. It looked just like my family's butler, in his same tuxedo and cloak of calm. "He told me how you wouldn't be returning to New York for a while, but that you would want your things."

"Bruce?"

He nodded. "Good to see you, Master Goldsmith."

"Why are you here?" I peered into his eyes. Was he a robot? A clone? He looked fine, exactly as I remembered him.

"Mr. Cristo invited me," he said, as if it was the most obvious thing in the world. "Of course, I wouldn't have left my duties, but he assured me you would come here." He paused. "Is this acceptable to you?"

"No—I mean, I guess so."

"You look tired, Master Goldsmith." Bruce gave me his knowing look. "Is there anything I can do for you?"

"He's had a long day," Don said. "Why don't you get some rest, Eli? I'll send for you once the baby is born."

"Okay." I was his prisoner, but at least I'd get a moment away from him.

He walked out and didn't look back.

After I was sure he was gone, I stepped warily into the

room. Two familiar chairs were by a window. Before, they'd been in the parlor in New York. I'd sat in one of them for a week, mourning my father's death. It seemed like an appropriate place to sit again.

I sat down and gazed outside over rocky hills. I preferred the view over Central Park. I closed my eyes, trying to collect myself. I wanted more than anything to be with Naomi.

"Sorry to disturb you," Bruce said. "Are you hungry, thirsty?"

I opened my eyes and shook my head. "This is all hard to believe."

"I agree, Master Goldsmith. Mr. Cristo's generosity knows no bounds."

"Generosity?"

Bruce glanced down at the chair beside mine. "May I?"

"Yes, please, of course."

He sat and folded his hands elegantly in his lap. His warm brown eyes showed great energy despite his age. "The last I heard from you," he began, "you were in Geneva. I watched the events there. I voted for Mr. Cristo, of course."

"I was there."

"At *the* United Nations' headquarters?"

I nodded.

"What an honor! But—" His brow lowered. "Those radical Muslims ruined it. Thank goodness for Mr. Cristo's drones defending the city. Otherwise who knows how many people might have died from their attack. The news says the Mahdi is still alive."

"I know."

He studied me curiously. "How did you get out of Geneva? Why didn't you come home? It has been so very empty."

"I'd rather not talk about it. Not here."

Bruce bowed his head. "Of course. My apologies, Master Goldsmith. Would you like me to go now?"

"No, it's fine . . . you were going to tell me why Mr. Cristo has been generous."

"Yes, yes. He visited New York yesterday. You can imagine my surprise when he arrived at our door. He told me you were going to be staying with him for a time. He said you were going to carry on your father's work."

"And what work is that?"

"Mr. Cristo didn't explain. But surely it relates to the UN's financing. This war is going to cost the world dearly."

"War?"

"I see you have been disconnected." An odd eagerness flickered in Bruce's eyes. "After the Mahdi led the attack in Geneva, Mr. Cristo invited the people to vote again. I was in Babylon at the time, but he reached me there. It was an easy choice. The Mahdi and his people must be eliminated if Mr. Cristo's vision is to succeed. His drones will first—"

"Wait. You were in Babylon?"

"Of course, Master Goldsmith. Why wouldn't I be? There has been very little to do with you gone. It is such a beautiful place. I've never felt so . . . carefree."

"But you're not in Babylon now."

"Obviously." He smiled. "When Mr. Cristo came and told me you'd be here, I had to help coordinate the move. The androids did the work, of course, and they'll be serving you here. I just couldn't miss a chance to see you again. You're the only family I have left," he sighed, "unless I'm in Babylon, that is. I guess I wanted to say goodbye."

"Don't go back there, Bruce."

He laughed, glancing down at his body. "Why would I stay in this old body when I can have my young, strong body back? No, Mr. Cristo is right, he has created a much better way for us."

"It's all an illusion. A lie."

"I'm sorry, Master Goldsmith, but I can't agree with that. I've been there. It's as true as anything I've ever seen. Mr. Cristo will take care of us."

"*Mr. Cristo* is the devil."

Bruce lurched to his feet. "You can't mean that!"

"I know it." I rose and met his hard stare. "I've seen him for what he really is."

"Is this about your visions?" he said accusingly. "Your father warned me about those. Have you been taking your medicine?"

My fists started shaking. "What did my father say?"

"He said you were crazy, like your mother."

"And you?" I asked through gritted teeth.

"I think your father was a wise man."

"Don manipulated him."

"And who manipulated you, Eli?"

I had no answer. He never called me Eli.

"Your mother?" he asked, his voice wavering like my friend Charles's had months ago. "The woman whose tumor gave her visions? The diseased seer?"

I fought against the urge to shove the man. "Get out."

"What's wrong, Eli?" He was smirking as he stepped back. Only then did I notice the thread of darkness snaking up his legs.

God help him, I prayed. "What happened to you?"

"I did what I could to help you."

The shadow twisting around him pulsed. *Listen to me*, it whispered, and I replied, *No, no, no!*

"Are you okay?" Bruce asked.

"No!" I shouted. *In the name of Jesus Christ, leave him!* The shadow froze, as if sensing my unspoken words. The darkness faded and was gone. He suddenly looked older. "Bruce?"

"This is goodbye." His voice was sad, more like himself, as he backed away.

"Wait, don't go. What happened?"

He stopped in the doorway. "I let Mr. Cristo's machines clone me. I let him into my precept." He shook his head. "I should've stayed in Babylon. Mr. Cristo is right. His world is pleasant. This world is pain." He turned to go. "You'll learn, Eli. You'll learn."

"Goodbye, Bruce." But he was already gone.

AFTER BRUCE LEFT, I paced around every inch of the room. I studied the marble floor, the ornate rugs. No sign of shadow. Whatever had touched Bruce was gone. Everyone was gone. I was alone.

The things from home were no comfort. It was all too strange. I went back to the mourning chair. I began to pray. I didn't know how or what to say, but my feelings raged. Fear. Anger. Loss. *Why would you allow this? Bruce was a good man. WHY?*

I didn't hear anything. There was no dream, no vision, no hope. I was trapped. How could I be any use in the devil's hands? Maybe it was just a matter of time before I'd have evil infecting me like it did Bruce.

No. I threw the thought away. I prayed harder.

Minutes passed in silence. Maybe an hour.

I was feeling desperate and exhausted when Don appeared in the doorway to my room. "The doctor tells me all went well. Ready to visit?"

I nodded and joined him. As we walked back along the same halls, questions came to me, starting with: "How did you make Bruce into a believer?"

Don glanced at me, amused. "Wasn't that difficult."

"He never liked technology. Now he's been to Babylon. He's always been a loyal caretaker, but not go-to-Babylon-and-fly-to-the-Middle-East loyal."

"Everyone has a price," Don said, as we reached a wide flight of red-carpeted stairs. We began walking up them.

"So . . . what was your price?"

Don paused mid-step and turned to me. "You want to play games?"

"I want to know what your price was."

"You have no idea what you're asking."

"I will when you answer."

"I have no price. I never did. I'm my own price and prize and purpose."

"You said everyone has a price."

"Everyone but me. I was the exception from the start, and I'll always be. That's why I rule here."

Deeper, I thought, *go deeper.* "And what about the baby? Does he have a price?"

Don stepped closer to me. He put his hand on my shoulder, and it felt like a shock to my system, like a knife severing the light that fed me the questions. But I stood my ground on the stairs. Don looked surprised, as if he'd expected a different reaction. "You've changed."

I nodded.

He put his face right into mine. His slitted irises bored into me. "It's not too late," he said. "I know my enemy taunts you with salvation. It is a lie. He tries to make great ones like us bow down. Not here, Elijah. This is MY world. And in my world, the weak bow before the great."

He released me and continued up the stairs. I followed him, my legs and my mind woozy. We reached a hallway with the sanitized whiteness of a hospital. No doctor, or any other human, was in sight.

We walked halfway down the hall and entered another door. It was a small, spotless room with a single bed. Naomi was on it. Two androids stood by her side. The robots must have removed every trace of a birth—except the baby.

Naomi held him to her breast, peering down at him. Their pale skin glowed together, pulsing with life in the bare room. It almost looked natural and normal.

"Well done," Don said.

She looked up with fatigue in her bloodshot eyes. "I won't let you touch him." She clutched the boy protectively.

Don moved closer. "I have no interest in touching him, but I need to see his face." He waved to me. "Come, Eli, have a look."

I went to Naomi's other side and put my hand on her shoulder assuringly. She met my gaze with a faint smile. I kept my eyes on hers.

"Hold him out, let me see," Don motioned.

Naomi didn't budge.

"You want to do this the hard way?"

Naomi's face was determined, but tears filled her eyes. "What do you want from him?"

Don smiled at her. "It's no mystery. You believe Jesus was the son of God, born in a manger and all that?"

Naomi nodded. The baby boy was quiet, peaceful in her arms.

"And you think he saved your soul?"

"Yes." She sounded certain.

Don shook his head. "He damned all of you to a life of groveling, tattered rags. His followers are like beggars tramping around the earth, seeking to rob the great souls of their vitality. Just look at you two. Where would you be right now without me? Still hiding in some dirty cave?"

"We would be free," I said.

Don's gaze swung slowly to me. "You believe that lie? My enemy wants suffering, obedient slaves. If you want freedom, follow me. You would have power beyond your dreams. Wealth and fame and comfort unknown to any before you."

"Man cannot serve two masters," Naomi said.

Don bent closer to Naomi and brushed back a strand of hair from her forehead. "You serve only me, and our son. I will give him what the enemy never could— dominion on this earth."

"What have you done to my baby?"

Don stroked her cheek smoothly. "That's what I need to see."

Her resolve crumbled before my eyes. Maybe it was Don's power, or just exhaustion, but she gently unfurled her arms around the boy. She turned him just enough for Don to see his face.

Don froze, then staggered back, his mouth clammed shut. He eyed Naomi uncertainly, accusingly. But a moment later his composure was back—all the arrogant anger a man could hold.

He stormed out of the room without another word.

I sat beside Naomi on the bed. I put my hand gently on her shoulder. "I've never seen Don like that. He must think something went wrong. What was it?"

She smiled up at me weakly, then motioned to the baby. "Look. He's perfect."

I glanced down at the boy. He had big round eyes like Naomi's and a head of dark hair. His face twisted as if he were about to cry, but when Naomi held him tight again, he sighed, eyes closing.

7

I STOOD IN the burning desert again. The fires raged, warming me, heating me, burning me. I smelled my flesh and my hair searing. I screamed out in pain.

Look up.

A light descended from the sky. A white throne, bigger and brighter than the earth. But this time a speck of dark rose up to meet it. The two looked destined to meet overhead, to explode against each other.

When I woke up, Naomi was peering down at me. I'd fallen asleep on the chair in her room. Her golden hair was like a curtain shielding me from the night and from the world. I wondered if she could protect me from those desert flames.

She leaned close to my ear. "You were groaning in your sleep. What did you see? Whisper it. They won't hear us."

I glanced at the motionless androids along the walls. Maybe she was right. Don could have sensors in the chair, or anywhere else, but he'd already shown he wasn't in complete control. I pulled her close and spoke softly into her ear, telling her every detail I could.

"I think it's about judgment," she said when I finished. Even in the darkness, concern was plain on her face.

"What kind of judgment?"

"The final judgment—when the living and the dead will be judged, each one of them, according to what they've done. Was anyone on the throne?"

"I couldn't tell. It was too far away. I would've burned before it came close enough to see."

She shook her head. "I don't think so. That's not how it's supposed to work."

"What do you mean?"

"The end of times. All those flames—were they like a lake?"

"It was a desert. Not a trace of water in sight."

"But maybe the desert was a dried-up lake? A lake of fire?"

"I guess that's possible. Why?"

"Revelation says that Death and Hades will be thrown into a lake of fire."

"Death and Hades?" I didn't remember that from what I'd read before, on the boat with Ronaldo. "It doesn't make any sense. Is Don supposed to be all of that? Even the Greek god of the underworld?" I laughed a little at the thought of him in a toga.

"Shhh," she whispered.

41

"Sorry." I'd let my voice rise. But it was too late now. The baby began to cry.

Naomi rose from the chair and shuffled over to the basinet by her bed. She reached down and picked him up. The crying immediately stopped, like a valve turned off, as she carried him back to the bed.

I turned away as she began to nurse him. "Want me to go?"

"Not really," she said, her voice weary, "but maybe it's best. Get some sleep, then see what you can learn about this place. I won't be able to do much for a few days."

I stood. "There must be some reason why we're here. I'll see what I can find, and I'll be back first thing in the morning."

"We'll miss you." Her lips curled into a grin. "Come back safe, okay? Pray as you go."

"I'll try."

She waved goodbye, then gazed down at the baby. She cradled it with the tender love of a mother, as if he was a normal infant, one with no trace of Don. As I walked out, I wondered if that was possible. Don had implanted the embryo, but then, he hadn't been the last one to touch her. On Patmos, Jesus had pressed his hand on her forehead. Had he done more than bring her back to life? Had he somehow healed the child?

I headed to my room under the watchful eyes of androids and shadows. Jesus and Patmos and light seemed so far away. This place was like a continuing nightmare. I slid into bed and sleep.

Now I was the infant. My Mom had me clutched to her

chest. I stared up at her chin, her face. I knew we were soaring over Jerusalem, but I didn't want to look. Everything would be safe as long as I kept my eyes on Mom.

She looked down at me. Her face was serious. "It's time for you to see."

She turned my infant body to face out. Dozens of towers reached into the sky like spindly fingers grasping for the heavens. As we flew closer to one of them, I saw it was no ordinary building. Where there should have been windows, it had capsules stacked along its sides. Thousands, maybe millions, of egg shapes large enough to hold a human body.

Babylon. But it was empty.

"Not even the devil knows what he does," my Mom said.

I tried to speak. I tried to ask why the eggs were empty. The babble of a baby came out of my lips.

Still, my Mom nodded, understanding. "The devil tries to bend the laws of nature. They do not bend. Push hard enough against them, and they'll break."

She soared straight down along the tower's side. I had the same flying sensation that I'd had in ISA training, in that drone in Shanghai almost a year ago. Except this, even in a dream, was no simulation. It was real. Horror hit me as I saw the ground . . . and the corpses stacked at the tower's base.

"Many will jump," my Mom said. "They will despair without the obscuring lens of technology."

Without Babylon. I understood. But how would Don lose control of it? And what was I supposed to do?

My Mom carried me ahead, along an empty street through the ancient parts of Jerusalem. We landed in the plaza before the Dome of the Rock. Its octagonal shape and round, golden top dominated the temple mount at the heart of the old city.

A man suddenly stood before us in blazing white, a man with wings. "Does the child have faith?"

My Mom nodded. "Elijah will believe, he will speak."

The angel stepped aside, expressionless, and Mom carried me past him. I had the sense of stepping out of the light and into a cave. The dragon appeared ahead, perched on top of the Dome, watching us approach. It gripped my uncle Jacob in one of its claws, and Aisha in the other. I started to cry, a helpless infant cry.

My Mom set my body down on the ground before the dragon. She knelt over me and looked into my eyes. "I cannot take you further than this. Save Aisha from the dragon. Tell Jacob I was right—it was the Messiah who caught the roof above his daughter."

I tried to nod. I tried to understand.

"You must fulfill your calling on your own." She wiped a tear from my baby cheek. Then she turned and left me.

I tried to watch her go, but my mind was trapped in the helpless infant body. I couldn't move. I couldn't avoid seeing the dragon above me.

The black creature bowed his neck down, revealing Don. He climbed off the dragon's back and glided to me.

He picked me up and dangled me before the dragon's eyes. The dragon stretched out its jaws. Down its throat was the purest black I'd ever seen. Don tossed me into the vicious mouth, and the dragon swallowed me whole. I slid down into the blackness. But inside, deep in the belly, there was a light. It pressed against me. The light was another child.

Naomi's son. He glowed brighter, then brighter still.

I wanted to cringe back from its dazzling light, but I couldn't move. The light strained against the blackness around us. The pressure built and built, making my ear drums throb. Then they popped, exploded. The light shattered the dragon, the dream, and everything else.

THE NEXT MORNING I had a dream hangover. I sat up in bed and rubbed my eyes, trying to focus on what was real from the day before. It was nearly as strange as my dreams.

Maybe a shower would help me think straight. I stumbled out of bed and made my way to the ornate bathroom. It was all white marble and steel and glass. I couldn't see cameras, but I had no doubt they were here. Don wouldn't leave anything to chance.

I quickly shed my clothes and stepped into the shower chamber. Robotic arms sprayed water over me, scrubbed me, then washed me clean. I felt like a car rolling through a car wash.

An android was waiting for me when I stepped out. Its

dark glass eyes looked down on me stoically. It held out a black suit and red tie. Like Don's.

I grabbed a towel and wrapped it tight around my waist. The thought of a suit Don had picked made me gag. "Something else," I commanded. "What about the clothes I came in?"

"The President offers you these," the android replied.

"I don't want them."

"I will dress you if needed." The robot's voice was hard, its body didn't budge. I didn't need any help to imagine it jabbing a needle into my neck and then forcing the clothes onto my unconscious body. Better not to test it.

"Fine. I'll do it." I grabbed the suit. "Now get out."

The robot bowed and marched through the door. No emotion. Just constant surveillance, insistence, and power.

I put on the suit and the tie, but avoided the mirror. I didn't need it to remind me how much I looked like Don.

When I stepped out of the room, the android spoke to me. "Naomi has been moved. I will show you the way."

"Why was she moved?"

"Follow me."

The android's four mechanical legs sprang into motion, and I hurried after it. We didn't go far. Don's minions had moved her and the baby to a room just down the hall from mine. Her quarters had marble walls and golden fixtures. Four androids were stationed in the corners. Nurses. Or guards. A luxurious prison.

The bed in the center of the room was immense. The sheets were silky red. Naomi was reclined with the baby cradled in her arms, basking in the sunlight that poured through the tall windows. Her gold-honey locks streamed down on the boy. He looked blissful as she dragged her hair over his face. He could have been the luckiest baby in the world. But I knew better, because I knew who his father was.

"Good morning." I sat on the foot of the bed.

Naomi looked me up and down. "Nice suit, but the tie's a little much for my taste."

"An android left me little choice." I pulled at the knot and tossed the tie to the floor. "How was the rest of the night?"

"Long," she sighed. "Remind me, we've been here seven years now?"

I smiled. "One day, I think."

"Right . . . ."

"You're exhausted. How can I help?"

"The androids are actually taking care of me. But they're watching everything we do. We've got to get out."

I nodded. "Haven't found any exits yet, but I'll work on it."

The baby stirred, letting out a slight whimper.

"Shhh," Naomi soothed, motioning for me to come closer. She whispered, "Can you take him to the crib?"

I moved to her side. She held up the bundle of cloth and baby. I took him gently. It felt surreal.

As I carried him and set him down in the crib beside Naomi's bed, I prayed the swaddled child would stay asleep. It was a small prayer, an answered prayer.

I turned back on tip-toes and joined Naomi. We each laid on our sides, facing each other, our noses inches away. We pulled the sheet over our heads. Her eyes almost made me forget what was going on around us. Almost.

"I think it's better when you do that," she whispered. "He can sense when a machine is holding him."

"Maternal androids got nothing on me."

Her smile was like a kiss of the sun.

"What's his name?" I asked.

She hesitated. "I feel like I shouldn't say it until we're out of here."

"Why? What if that doesn't happen?"

"It's going to happen."

"I know we'll eventually be free, but—" I picked my words carefully. "We don't know exactly what will happen to your son."

"Maybe not, but God will work this for the good. He will defeat Don's plans. It doesn't matter how my baby came into this world. He's mine. He's innocent."

"What about the non-Naomi-half of his chromosomes?" *Could Jesus cure the baby of that?*

"Have you seen anything unusual about him?"

"He's growing fast, for one thing. You were pregnant only six months. As far as I know, most babies aren't this big the day after they're born. It's like he's supercharged."

"Don enhanced his genes. But his soul is still bright. You saw Don's reaction when he saw him."

"Yeah, surprise. Anger. You think Don will just let this boy stay normal?"

"This isn't about what Don wants. God is in control."

"So? God has always been in control. And the world has witnessed a million evils. The drone wars. The Holocaust. God's own people slaughtered women and children to take the Promised Land. That's some track record."

"We will win this battle." She sounded defiant, as confident as my mother in the dream. "God will answer my prayers. My son *will* stay clean."

"I hope you're right." Doubt tinged my voice as I thought of what Don had said about *his son* and of the baby in the pit of the dragon's belly. "Maybe if you name him, that will help him have an identity separate from his father."

Her face tightened, the way it did when she got angry, righteously angry. "He *has* a separate identity. Don will *not* have the final say. We all have a father in God." She poked at my chest. "Even the fatherless."

My mouth opened, but I did not know how to respond.

She put her hand on my cheek. "That hurt you. I'm sorry, I didn't mean . . . I haven't slept."

"It's okay. I understand." Her apology helped.

"It's hard to think straight." She breathed out deeply. "You had a good idea."

"About the name?"

She nodded. "But not yet, not here. Besides, that's not why you showed up here this morning without taming your hair." Her fingers played in my disheveled curls, untangling knots of tension in my head. "Without you, I would be alone with my baby in the devil's lair. We've got to find a way out. We've got to pray for God to be with us, to show us what to do."

"I'll explore the palace. See what I can find."

"Good. But stay a little longer?"

"Of course."

She smiled and closed her eyes. Her breathing deepened and slowed. I watched her, loved her, and prayed for some way out.

9

THE DAY PASSED with me in and out of fitful sleep. In the late afternoon, I left Naomi and the baby and started exploring. I walked past the door to my room and turned down a new palace hall. It took my breath away. The floor was polished black marble with a single stretch of lush red carpet. The hall was so long that the lines almost converged to a point in the distance. Down the whole stretch, android sentries stood motionless a few feet apart, like medieval suits of armor in a castle.

I made my way along the hall. The dark colors and robot eyes weighed on me, but not as much as the overwhelming feeling of a presence. I didn't see demons. I didn't see angels. But out of the corner of my eye, always just out of sight, there were vapors and mists and clouds of black darker than shadow. The black had forms and it moved. Whenever I sensed it reaching for me, like grasping fingers, I'd yank away and snap my head toward it. But then nothing would be there. Not even a shadow. It toyed with me, playing on my vision.

I forced myself to walk the entire perimeter of the palace, praying with every step, *God be with me, show me what to do, be with me, show me* . . . . Down the north hall, then the east, the south, and up again to my quarters in the west—a perfect square. Each hall seemed the same, both in length and color and evil. But something was different about the east hall. The darkness wasn't as heavy there.

I'd lingered in that hall. I'd tried opening doors, going up the stairs. Yet every time I veered away from the red carpet, the androids would block my path. They didn't negotiate. They were unhackable without my precept connected, and even if I could have hacked one, that would have left thousands more to stop me.

Eventually I gave up and returned to Naomi. She was asleep, so I went back to my room and fell into bed.

I awoke with a start some hours later. My room was empty, but I still couldn't shake the sense of being watched. I decided to venture out again. I couldn't bear to walk the whole square palace. Its darkness was too heavy, too exhausting. The night sky through the palace's arched windows was more inviting. I needed some fresh air.

I found a small balcony off the north hallway. The sentries on either side let me pass, probably because the balcony allowed no way out. Two urns holding palm trees framed the view high over the barren landscape. I leaned on the golden railing and gazed up. In the center of the star-filled night, the slightest sickle of the moon sliced a gash in the blackness.

What now, God?

I waited in quiet. I heard nothing.

Are you listening? How can I get Naomi out? Show me.

I closed my eyes for a long time. I opened them. Still nothing.

Where are you, Lord? Was that you in my dream—the one with the sun? Will that happen? What now?

Nothing. Silence. The night sky. *Am I talking to myself?* The stars teased me, as if those balls of burning gases had any answers. But then one flashed. Or had it? I could have sworn one of the stars had sparked, as if exploding a billion miles away. Now the spot was dark.

There! Another star blinked brightly and then disappeared. Not like a shooting star. Like a bone-dry leaf blazing for an instant before it burned itself out. I kept my eyes peeled, but it didn't happen again.

God, is that you? Was that supposed to mean something? The dreams, the stars—are you trying to warn me?

No answer. More silence.

My dreams seemed more real than my prayers. Maybe I was going crazy—locked in Don's palace with every comfort I could want and every terror I didn't, unsure of what had happened to Michael and the order, unable to help Naomi, tired and weak.

I fell to my knees, desperate. *God, what do you want from*

me?

TRUST. WAIT.

An answer. Two words. I didn't hear them aloud, but I knew it wasn't from me. My mind wouldn't have come up with those words. The last thing I wanted to do was wait. But if that was the command, I would do it.

Thank you. I will trust and wait. What else?

Silence.

I'd take what I could get. *Trust* in God. Didn't I already? *Wait.* Did I have any other choice? How long did I have to—

"The crescent moon," said Don's voice.

It made me jump to my feet, and almost out of my skin. He was beside me, from out of nowhere, and his dark eyes fixed on me. It was like he'd heard God's words and come.

"Isn't it beautiful?" He gazed out into the night. "Know what it means?"

"The moon?" I tried to sound composed.

"Yes."

"I guess it means the moon completed another orbit around earth."

"Funny." Don turned to me with his unnerving grin. "It makes no sense that your kind would have humor."

"Why?"

His sudden laugh made me cringe. "How long will you pretend to not know me?"

"You're Donatello Cristo, the President of the UN."

"A name, a title. An insult for the god of this world.

We are being honest, Eli. Would you dare insult me again?"

"Why do you care what I say?"

"Because apparently my enemy cares." He paused and looked back toward the moon. "I asked you a question. What does *this* crescent moon mean?"

"It would mean a new month in a lunar calendar."

"You're getting closer. This will be the most important month in the earth's history."

"The last month?"

"Yes, my final victory." His knuckles were white as he gripped the balcony's rail. "Tonight my army attacks. The Muslims have just started their holy month celebration, Ramadan. They think my sights are only on Jerusalem, but I save that jewel for the end. My forces, sharp as this sickle moon, will first slice the legs off Persia. It will fall and burn in days. Then I will finish with Jerusalem, and all will worship me. Trust in me, Eli, or you will die like the rest of my enemies."

I was trembling—some foul combination of fear and anger and uncertainty. "Why are you telling me this?"

He held me with his smile, teeth bared, and for a moment I thought he might swallow me like the dragon. But then he answered, "He is not the only one who cares about souls. You think we are so different—the maker and me?"

"Yes."

"Just because he came first?" Don sighed. "A common mistake. The clouds give birth to lightning, but that does not make the lightning anything less. No, the lightning is more, just as I am more. We all crave to be worshiped. He just wants worship in a new place, with only his chosen. I would welcome all."

I felt Don's words wrapping around me, soft and silky lies that bind like steel. My mind came to the question that had led me to God in the first place. "But why?" I asked. "Why does God want that?"

"It doesn't matter why. What matters is what you do and what you feel. He would make you a slave to his law. I will make you free."

In a virtual test tube. "I've been to Babylon," I said flatly.

His smile faltered, then his lips turned up again. "I want you on my side, Eli. You know you're not like other people. You are to them what I am to the angels. And you saw how Michael fared." He clasped my shoulder, tight. "We can rule this earth together. Don't give that up for some vague promise of *trust and wait.*"

A shudder ran down my spine. *He had heard.* I stuffed my fear down. "I'll think about it."

"Time is running short. You have one more month."

A month stuck here? "If I am free, will you let me leave?" I asked. "Naomi, too?"

"She must care for my son, and I promised you would stay with her. I know, you grow restless. So do I. If you want to protect Naomi's life—" he paused, just long enough for me to understand his threat— "then you'll join me in this battle. I have drones with more power than you've ever seen. Syncing to them is like harnessing a hurricane."

He said that as if I should be excited about the power, and as if I had a choice. I had to protect Naomi. Maybe I could at least learn something to help us escape. "I'm interested in these drones."

He smiled, glorious and inviting. "I will send you information. Take control of your own fate instead of groveling to others. Naomi's life is in your hands."

I nodded, unsure of what to say. *Trust. Wait.* I looked back at the moon, as if it held any answers. The night suddenly felt very quiet, very dark, and very lonely.

I turned back to Don, but he was gone.

10

DON WAS NOWHERE to be seen in the following days. They passed in a blur of midnight feedings, 4 a.m. cries, and bleary-eyed, shuffling steps from Naomi's room to mine. I wandered the halls but found no spot unguarded. I began getting used to the constant companionship of androids. My dreams came every night—the same ones, but each a slightly different iteration, each full of terror and confusion and hope. Naomi and I had no contact with the outside world. We heard nothing from God. Nothing from the order. Nothing from Don.

One morning a tablet of information arrived. Its thin glass frame sat on the foot of my bed when I woke up. I'd slept through whatever snuck into my room and delivered it. The thought of some android leaning over me in my sleep made me want to shower.

I didn't touch the tablet. Not yet. I went through the robotic showering ritual, put on another black suit—the only clothes available. I went back into the bedroom and hesitated over the tablet. It was in the same place, a flat sheet of circuits. It couldn't do any harm if I left it alone. But I couldn't use it that way. Naomi and I weren't getting anywhere on our own. I picked it up and walked out.

I passed the two androids waiting by the door. They didn't follow, they never did. They had a thousand other machine-eyes to watch the palace.

I went straight to Naomi. We shared our good mornings: as usual, nothing new had happened during the night. More lost sleep. More of the same dreams. The baby was snoozing.

"Look." I held up the tablet, glinting in the morning light. "It showed up last night. I bet it's the drone info." I'd told her all about the conversation with Don.

Naomi's tired eyes fixed on the tablet. She motioned for me to join her on the bed, as we did when we wanted to avoid being overheard. She whispered, "I still don't like this."

"Shouldn't we at least see the information?"

She leaned closer, her breath warm on my ear. Her voice was soft but firm. "It will be designed to deceive."

"I know," I replied quietly, "but we can pray for God's help while we review it."

"We should pray, but it's not that simple. We're not supposed to fling ourselves into temptation, and Don could make this irresistible. We may not know what he's up to, but we know he's full of lies. I don't like the idea of you rebooting your precept, much less syncing with one of his drones. You can't leave me alone here. You can't go into this war, even if your intentions are to help the order. Don won't let that happen anyway."

"It's just my mind. My body will stay here."

A slight smile touched her lips, but not her eyes. "You think I want your body without your mind? Besides, Don's drones will be more complex than what we used in ISA-7. You know the risks if your drone is taken out."

I thought of the Captain losing his mind and diving out of a skyscraper. The deeper we went in, the worse the shock if we got ejected. "I know the risks," I said. "I'll avoid a complete sync."

"Better to avoid syncing all together."

"Let's at least see what information Don provided. We may have a chance to use it, even if I don't sync." I put on my most convincing smile. "I promise I won't go unless it's necessary."

"Nice try, pretty boy. What would make it *necessary* for you to go?"

"If God tells me to do it."

"You'll limit it to that?"

Trust. Wait. "I promise."

We turned to lay on our backs, our sides pressed together, as I held up the glass tablet over us. It was as thin as paper, and not much heavier.

"You ready?" I asked.

"Almost," she said, closing her eyes. "God, give us

vision now. Protect us from evil, help us resist temptation, show us your will. Amen." Her eyes opened. "Go ahead."

I activated the tablet. The screen expanded into a holographic ocean before us. It felt like we were soaring backwards, just above clear blue water. Waves lapped gently over a wide stretch of whitish-yellow sand. Palm trees dotted the crescent coast, and an immense city loomed in the distance.

The view froze. The focus sharpened on still figures between the ocean and the palms. Thousands of soldiers wore armored suits in the dull color of desert camouflage. They formed a line three men deep, stretching the entire screen along the beach. I hardly would have seen them except for their guns. Lasers, missiles, and artillery. They had enough firepower to seize a nation, and all of it was aimed toward the water.

As the soldiers held their positions and the gentle waves rolled in, an overlay of text appeared: *November 23, 2066, 9:34 am. Outside Dubai.* That was about two weeks ago, not long after Don had told me war would begin.

The text faded. The waves lapped. The palm trees blew gently in the wind.

The view spun out over the water again. Something lit up a hundred feet out, like a mirror catching the sun. Then dozens of mirrors. Each one rising higher and stirring the calm ocean around it. Giant metallic bodies emerged from the depths, marching toward the coast.

For a moment, no soldiers fired. The line of machines advanced on the line of men, the distance closing. Then, in unison, a line of missiles flew from the advancing creatures. The streams of white clouds, perfectly parallel, could have been beautiful.

The missiles hit—not the men, but a shield. They exploded against an invisible bubble just above the men. It must have been a thermal shield like the one over Washington, DC. As the burning missiles fell into the water, the shield blinked away, just for an instant. The men on the shore unleashed a flurry of shots at the machines. Then the shield was back.

The soldiers' salvo hit the metal beasts like a wave. Several of the giant creatures stumbled. A few fell, crashing into the water, but most still advanced, steady and unflinching. They reached the crashing waves, closing in on the men, before they bumped against the invisible wall. The men stood their ground as the machines each reached out with artificial hands. Spindly, metallic digits prodded at the shield, as if searching for a weakness.

The unseen wall held. The men had to be frantic inside, but they looked as calm as statues while the drones continued their work—their masterminds probably trying to hack whatever code was controlling the shield. In the moment of equipoise, the screen's view zoomed away, lifting like a bird on the sea breeze.

The water stirred again, farther out this time. Another metal beast began to rise and advance. This one dwarfed the others. It was maybe twice their size, with four legs instead of two. Seven heads grew from its hulking frame, looking every direction at once. The machine moved faster and faster, surging out of the water and charging at the line of men. It slammed against the shield, cracking it from top to bottom. It reared back and slammed forward again. This time the shield shattered.

The men opened fire.

The machines returned it.

Within chaotic minutes of explosions and screams, the beach was covered in blood. No man remained standing, and interspersed among their bodies were heaps of fallen metal. The view zoomed onto the face of the largest machine. It roared out a victory cry like a lion.

The video faded out and text appeared: *Persian casualties: 166,449. UN casualties: 7. Press to continue.*

I didn't press the button.

Naomi breathed heavily beside me. "That was enough," she whispered. "If Don can do this without you, why would he ask you to join him? How could this be anything other than a trap?"

"The Mahdi's men won't continue like this. I bet they're changing strategies. Maybe going into hiding. Think about an army of Aishas. Guerrilla warfare. Terrorist attacks. Not every battle will go so easily for Don."

"Maybe," Naomi said, "but still, why would Don need you?"

"He knows our capacities for syncing with drones. He knows I'm one of the best." It wasn't bragging. Those were facts.

"And he knows you're aligned with the order now. He knows God is with you." Naomi took my hand in hers.

"Look, we both know you can sync with a drone, but so can I. Don wants me around to take care of his son, to be a mother he can parade around. But he doesn't *need* you. You're a threat, so why wouldn't he try to dispose of you?"

"If that's all he wanted, he would have killed me already."

"Okay, so what's he really after?"

I thought for a moment. I remembered what Ronaldo had said about Satan wanting to twist all that is good into evil. I remembered what the order had been saying all along about my role in this. If—for whatever reason—I was chosen by God to be His seer, did that mean His enemy would necessarily choose me, too, for whatever his purposes?

"What are you thinking?" Naomi pressed.

"Don's trying to twist God's plan."

"How? Which plan?"

"I'm not sure . . . it's God's plan, not mine. But it's probably whatever plan involves me seeing things no one else can see. It's whatever plan leads you to be the mother of Don's child, and for us to be here right now, together in the devil's palace. It's whatever plan makes me fall in love with you, and you with me." I squeezed her hands and stared into her eyes. "I think I'm supposed to trust that God will protect me in this, and then wait for him to show me what's next."

She went quiet, then pressed her eyes shut, as if praying. When they opened, she looked resolved. "I'll let you do this on one condition."

"What's that?"

"You tell me every detail of your training, of the drones, and of Don's mission. I want to know all of it."

I smiled. "The warrior mother. It's a deal."

She didn't smile back. "This isn't about us fighting. We have no strength on our own. We must pray constantly. But God must have put us here for a reason. The more we know, the better we can pray." She turned to the screen. "Let's see what's next."

11

I PRESSED THE glass tablet to continue the video. The battle scene was gone in the next frame, replaced by Beatriz's face. I hadn't seen the woman since Geneva. I hadn't missed her.

"Welcome, Elijah!" She spoke fast, full of excitement. "You have already seen the glory of our machines in battle, but they are so much more. They are masterpieces. They combine the best of mankind's creations. Powerful engines, impenetrable frames, and growing intelligence. They *could* operate independently, but it remains advisable to control them. Our futures are tied together. An advanced human mind can sync with dozens at a time. Don instructed me to give you a glimpse of my current harvest. Watch and learn."

The screen shifted to a city—my city, New York—but it spliced into a dozen different views. Each one was a thin sliver on the screen, and they sprang into motion at once. It was dizzying trying to follow them all. One sliver showed black metallic arms approaching a woman's body, apparently asleep on the bed of a tiny apartment. The arms stripped her clothes off and sheared her head bare. Then it gathered her body up like a bundle of wheat.

My eyes moved to another sliver. They showed another set of robotic arms lowering a man's body into a clear, egg-shaped chamber, like the one from Alexi's mansion. The next sliver showed the side of a building. It was familiar—an art deco tower from the block where I grew up. But it was not the same. The outside of the building had as many egg-shaped chambers as windows. Most of them were empty, but as I looked closer, I could see spider-like robots hauling bodies and laying them in the capsules.

Beatriz's word hit me with force: *a harvest.*

I scanned the other slivers of the screen. They all showed flurries of the same mechanical activity. Bodies being stripped clean, gathered up, hauled, and deposited in chambers. I wiped the cold sweat from my forehead. Was this the fate of those in Babylon?

Beatriz's face appeared again, filling the entire screen. "You see, these people have put their trust in Don, and they enjoy paradise without lifting a finger. With these beautiful creations, Don has eliminated work and replaced it with pleasure."

"Stop the video," Naomi said. "I can't watch this."

"Okay—" I reached for the screen.

"Hello, Naomi," Beatriz interrupted. "I did not see you there."

This was live! I spun the screen away.

I resisted the temptation to hurl the glass tablet against the wall, as awesome as it would have been to see this crazy woman shatter into a thousand pieces.

"What did you expect?" Beatriz asked. "Don has offered you a place of great privilege. He gives you an opportunity to ask me whatever you wish." She paused. "You might as well turn the screen back. I've already seen that Naomi is with you."

I glanced to Naomi at my side. She nodded and mouthed, *learn what you can. I'll pray.*

I slowly spun the screen around and met Beatriz's fanatic gaze.

"Go ahead," the woman said. "You have questions?"

"These people, are their minds in Babylon?"

She nodded. "We monitor their vitals to make sure they are healthy and happy. No one enters Babylon without choosing it. You should know by now, Don is a lover of freedom."

"Freedom? You are putting people in test tubes."

"You've been there, Elijah." Beatriz's eyes took on a devious smile as they turned to Naomi. "Was there anything unpleasant about the experience? Why don't you tell me what you saw?"

"Isn't it recorded somewhere? You probably know what I saw."

She shook her head. "I have my suspicions, but only Don has access to that data. We respect people's privacy. If the dwellers of Babylon feared their deepest desires could be known, they would hold back their desires. Don wants every person to have his or her deepest cravings satisfied. But that doesn't mean you can't tell us. Was Babylon unpleasant for you?"

The images from my brief time there were seared into my memory. I thought of Naomi on the bed, beckoning me to her tropical paradise. I thought of Jezebel. *Unpleasant* was the wrong word. It was flat-out wrong.

"Babylon is not reality," I said. "As powerful as our minds are, we cannot live without our bodies."

"That was the past," Beatriz replied. "Under Don's oversight, the machines can provide for our bodies. The flesh has always been a nuisance, holding humans back from their highest destinies."

"If that were true, why would you and Don choose to stay in the real world, in your bodies?"

"Good question." Her lips curled up, crinkling the lines of wrinkles around her eyes. "It is our sacrifice, on behalf of others, to remain here and ensure the world remains safe so that people may enjoy Babylon."

"So generous of you. Is that why you're killing anyone who refuses to enter Babylon?"

"Don is only defending what the people have chosen," she said. "We cannot allow a few fundamentalists to ruin what nearly everyone else in the world wants. But we force no one to enter Babylon. Each person chooses it for themselves. They may stay outside, as long as they acknowledge Don's authority."

"What's that supposed to mean?" I thought of the order—Chris, Ronaldo, and the others—hiding somewhere, probably in another cave. "How can they acknowledge his authority without entering Babylon?"

"You're a New Yorker, so consider a group in your state, the Amish. You know how they live in the United States, but remain separate from it?"

"Yes."

"Don tolerates that. This very second, many of the Amish are still on their lands, riding their carriages, growing their vegetables." Her voice held contempt. "They never accepted precepts in the first place, so they didn't even get a taste of Babylon. Of course, we would welcome them to join us, but as long as they stay within their territory and recognize that Don is their ultimate sovereign, they can carry on like farm animals."

"But the Muslims fight back," I said. "That's the difference?"

"It's far more than that. Anyone with a will to power is a threat to the peaceful world Don is creating."

Peaceful. Some word for war machines slaughtering thousands. I kept my calm. "What do you mean by will to power?"

"Anything that tries to set itself above Don and the greater good. The responsibility to maintain world order can be shouldered only by the greatest men and women. Don sees immense potential in you, Elijah Goldsmith. He told me that you've seen the dragon." She sounded genuinely impressed. "He said you saw Jezebel. He said you harnessed the Omega Project on the first try. Only a handful have had that opportunity, and fewer still have succeeded."

Was that jealousy in her voice? "So what's next?"

"Even you must train," Beatriz said. "Reconnect your precept, and the next training will be there for you."

"And if I don't?"

Beatriz paused as if taken aback. "Then I suppose you'll be left behind. You'll lose Don's favor. You'll probably die. But I don't think it will happen that way. My agents have had their eyes on you from the beginning. You're smart, Eli. Don's war machines have more power than anything you've experienced. If you prove yourself capable and loyal, then Don will honor you."

Her agents? It suddenly clicked that she ran ISA under Don. "I understand. How has Don honored you?"

Her face tightened. "Don gives to all as they deserve. He will wait for you, but not forever. The battle is underway."

"What about Naomi?"

"What about her?" Beatriz glanced at Naomi with disdain. "She's alive now, while she nurses the child. I suggest she enjoy the honor while it lasts. Not everyone can be our Lord's genetic match, but even that affords no permanent place at his side."

I turned to Naomi. She was biting her lip. She shook her head at me, as if telling me not to take the bait. I looked at Beatriz again.

"Reboot your precept," she said. "Instructions await there."

The screen's image went blank.

12

"SO WHAT NOW?"

Naomi rose up with her palms flat on the red sheets and her slender arms as support. Her beautiful face was like a gulp of fresh air after staring at Beatriz on the screen.

"He should be asleep for another hour," Naomi said softly, glancing to the cradle. "We'll be monitored, but I need a stretch—maybe somewhere outside, in the sun?"

"There's a courtyard nearby. Can you take stairs? Just two stories." She'd been walking within the first few days of the birth, but she hadn't ventured far from her room. No one had said she couldn't, but the androids' instructions were to rest as much as possible.

"I think so," she said, sliding out of bed and stretching her arms. "My body is feeling much better. Stronger."

"Great, let's go." We slipped out of the room. The baby didn't stir, but Naomi paused in the door between the two androids on guard.

She whispered to one of them. "Get me immediately if he wakes."

"Yes, Naomi," it replied.

She nodded. "Monitor?"

The robot's stomach slid open, producing a small flat screen from inside. Naomi took it. "This has worked when I shower," she said. "No reason it won't work now." She pressed the monitor's screen. It showed the baby. A glance back into the room confirmed it was the view from the eyes of the nearest android. Naomi took my arm and smiled faintly.

The androids didn't follow as we left. We made our way down a broad marble staircase, with Naomi seeming to gain confidence with each step. After passing through a long hall, I led us through the open door to an enclosed courtyard. It was immense, half the size of a soccer pitch, and magnificent in the mid-morning light. Paths crisscrossed in perfect geometry through the lush fruit trees and flowers. Small machines scurried around like dogs, watering and pruning the plants. It was hard to believe we were in the middle of a desert.

"Let's sit here." Naomi pointed to a bench under a tree with round, red apples begging to be picked.

"Remember the first time we sat on a bench together?"

She lowered to the bench gently. "I'll never forget it. You were the arrogant Jewish boy with the dark curls and the darker dreams."

"And you were the girl clothed with the sun—all beautiful and innocent and ready to make me spill my secrets. How'd you do that, by the way? I've never understood how you dragged my dream out of me."

"I felt like there was something special about you, so I prayed. I asked God to help me, to show what you were hiding." She grinned. "My prayers usually aren't answered quite so fast."

"And look where that led us."

She studied me quietly. "You think you could've avoided all this if I hadn't dragged you to meet the order?"

"I don't know." I hesitated, then smiled. "Either way, you're worth everything I've gone through—the dragon, the desert, Babylon, and now Don's palace. I'd do it all again. We're together now."

She took my hand. "You've changed, you know."

"It wouldn't have happened without you. And maybe Bart, and Chris, and Ronaldo, and . . . ."

She nodded, but her eyes said she'd moved to the next thought. She was studying the garden around us. She bent over and glanced under the bench, then she leaned close to my ear. "Think we're being overheard?"

"Maybe. There's a chance everything *can* be heard. Don's androids are walking recorders, and sensors are everywhere. But this seems at least as safe as your room." I met her green eyes. They were open wide, a little afraid. "What is it?"

She pressed close to my ear again. "We have to decide

about turning on your precept, and I've heard nothing from God. It makes me worried. What have you seen?"

I hesitated, careful with my words. "I've seen myself in Jerusalem, facing the dragon." Her body tensed, and I tried to assure her. "It's not much to go on, but I heard God clear as day: *trust and wait.* And before that, in the order's hideaway, Jesus told me to let my enemies give me quarter and then, *in the moment when the world listens, tell the world I am coming.* Well, here I am in Don's palace, and how can I speak to the world without my precept? It seems like I should take the opportunity."

"But this opportunity is from Don." Her voice dropped to the lowest whisper. "I told you, he doesn't need your help."

"Think about why he picked you as his woman clothed with the sun. He's taking God's story and trying to corrupt it. So, for whatever reason, if God picked me to see spiritual things and come to believe them, wouldn't his enemy want to twist that?"

"I guess so. But how?" She paused, fixing her eyes on mine.

I thought of how he'd used Charles's body as a puppet. "I bet he thinks he can tempt me to join him. And if that fails, he probably thinks he can just control me."

"That's right. So what are you going to do if you sync up to one of those killing machines and find yourself with no option but to slaughter a bunch of men or be killed?"

My voice came out steady: "I'll follow the Captain's path."

"That's *not* an option."

"We know Don will be defeated in the end. There's no guarantee I'll be around to see it." I thought of her son beside me—in the dragon. "There's no guarantee for any of us."

Naomi closed her eyes and breathed deeply. "All who believe in Him have a guarantee. And no one with that guarantee would take his own life. It's true we might suffer—like being trapped by Don—but I trust God's plan." Her eyes opened. "He called you to serve Him at the end."

Her steady faith made me smile. She'd just had the devil's baby, and yet here she was telling me to trust God. I didn't want to think about where I'd be without her. "You're right." I took her hands in mine. "I'm trying to serve Him, and I think that means connecting my precept. I have to join this fight."

She looked resigned to it, or maybe just tired. "You have to tell me everything you learn."

"I already agreed to that."

"Good." She yawned, then glanced down at the monitor, at the sleeping boy. "Let's head back. He'll be waking up soon."

"Still not going to tell me his name?"

She shook her head and stood. She began to reach her arms up, yawning again, but winced and dropped them to her side.

"You okay?"

"It still hurts a little," she admitted. "Can you grab one

of these apples for me?"

"Isn't that what Eve said to Adam?"

She laughed. "Something like that, but you're the one desperate to turn your precept on. I'm just hungry."

I picked two apples and handed her one. "Here, the forbidden fruit. Let me know what you learn about good and evil."

She looked up at the palace's tower looming high above us. "I already know more than I'd like."

13

LATER THAT DAY Naomi came to my room while the baby was sleeping again. We sat across from each other in the chairs by the window, overlooking the rocky desert hills. We talked more about Don's offer and Beatriz's message. We prayed. We asked God what it meant to trust and wait. We got no clear answer. I had waited for more guidance. I had waited until Don sent the instructions. And now I would trust. I would turn on my precept.

Three presses to the wrist and V was back.

My head suddenly felt doused in grease—slippery and tainted. My senses were sharper, but less real.

"Good afternoon, Elijah," V greeted with her cheerful voice. "Twenty-three days and four hours since last shutdown."

Was that all? I wondered. That had been in Jerusalem, with Brie from the order. She'd told me never to turn my precept on again. Was she right, or had things changed? Too late now.

V spoke in my mind. "You have thirty thousand six hundred forty-two messages, nine hundred twenty news briefings, and fifty-seven trainings. You also have—"

"Stop."

V stopped. That shouldn't have been comforting, but it was. At least V still obeyed. The messages and briefings could wait.

"Why did you tell it to stop?" Naomi asked. "You look scared."

"It was too much at once." I stared wide-eyed at her. With the influx of information from V, I'd forgotten I would get access to Naomi's vitals. It felt like so long since we had synced during ISA training. I checked her familiar digital presence in my mind. Her heart rate was normal, but her synapses were firing at 68% of her normal speed. She was exhausted.

"You've got to get more sleep," I said.

"I know. But . . . why are you looking at me like that? You still have my data from our sync?"

I nodded. "It's still there. Remember, Don's network keeps the data flowing even when precepts are off. More sleep, okay?"

"You ever try sleeping when there's a baby waking you up every two hours?" She put on her best attempt at a smile. "I'll be fine. What about your precept?"

"V auto-connected with the system, and she was about to report on my messages and everything."

"Stay focused," she said. "See if there's something from the order."

"Okay." I leaned back and closed my eyes. I instructed V to run a search for the names of anyone in the order. She came up with two results since I'd shut her down.

The first was a message from Chris—twelve days ago. V played the video. Chris's face was covered in sweat, like he'd been running. He was in a dark room. His face looked hollowed, lit by candlelight.

We lost Neo, he said. *Only four of us remain. But we will come for you. Stay safe, protect Naomi, and pray.*

That was it. The video blinked off. I opened my eyes.

Naomi hadn't moved. "What is it?"

I told her what Chris had said.

Her head fell into her hands. She was quiet, trembling. She eventually looked up. "I can't believe Neo's dead."

My thoughts drifted to the man's hideaway in Montana, and all the children he sheltered. "Chris didn't mention the kids."

Naomi sat up straight, as if willing herself out of pain, out of fear. "God will save them, if not on earth, then in heaven."

"If Chris or anyone tries to come, they won't stand a chance."

"Don't think like that." She sounded poised, assured— the news had changed something about her. "We must keep praying and keep going. What's the next message?"

I closed my eyes again. V played the next one.

It was Ronaldo, from only a few hours ago. He looked calm, with the same bright eyes as always. The wall behind him was the same color stone as the palace. He started speaking, relaxed.

They caught me, mon. I'd been bidin' time, hopin' to help, and I even got a drone to the palace. But the devil's watchin'. He followed the sync to my hideout. Maybe he knew all along. He certainly knows it all now. Ain't no more use tryin' to hide. They hauled me here. Looks like they'll be locking me up in the palace's east wing. Come soon.

"What happened?" Naomi asked as my eyes opened. Her voice reflected the excitement that was surely on my face.

"Ronaldo. He's here. Don caught him."

She bounced to her feet. "What else?"

"He said he's locked up in the east wing of the palace."

"Then what are we waiting for?"

"Don knows everything we do, everything we say here."

"He *can* know everything," she said, "but that doesn't mean he *does*. He's not omniscient. He can't monitor everything at the same time."

I glanced around my room at all the places where cameras could hide. "I'm not sure about that."

"Only God can do that."

"Or the devil with technology."

"We've got no choice." She held out her hand to me. "We'll be careful with what we say. Let's go."

"It has to be a trap."

"We're already trapped!" She pulled me out of the chair. "It's a long walk to the east wing, right?"

I nodded.

"Let's get baby boy. I'll bring him with us. Can you wait a little while?"

"Sure, I'll start the drone training while I wait."

She hesitated.

"I might as well, so we'll have more info for Ronaldo."

"Pray unceasingly." She turned to go, a bounce in her step for the first time in days. "See you soon."

14

V STARTED THE training, and everything changed.

My mind, my entire consciousness, felt like it was swirling through a pipe, out of my body and into somebody else's. I heard Don's voice before I could see anything.

"You are inside the most powerful machine in the universe. Let's see what you can do."

I opened my eyes. I was standing in a giant crater, larger than a football stadium. The crater was full of ramps and towers and vehicles, like some kind of mining operation. A line of smaller machines was facing me. No human was in sight.

In my mind, I lifted my arm. A massive metallic arm rose in front of me. It was thicker than a tree trunk.

I thought of clenching my fist. The arm's fist clenched.

I thought of taking a step, and I moved forward, the ground shaking beneath me. And so it went—my every thought mapped onto this enormous machine's movements.

But there was more. Every part of this body brought a menu of options. My fingers showed: Gun. Blade. Virus. Fire. Darkness.

Every part of me had options. Ways to destroy, it seemed.

I tried to think of a way out. There was no exit button. "Eject," I said.

Nothing.

"Reboot."

Don's laughter filled my mind. "You can leave when I let you. Pick a weapon."

I tried to keep my mind still, to not think. But I couldn't. It was like there was something else sharing the machine with me. Not someone. But something . . . *other*. It was strong and close. The *other* seemed to sway my thoughts like a wind blowing a leaf.

Stay still, I thought, but I couldn't. My mind drifted to the blade option. A gleaming sword the size of a flag pole slid out of the robotic finger. With a flicker of thought, I swung the blade at a line of towers. Four of them split in half and toppled over. Steel beams sliced like butter.

Then my mind went to *fire*. Suddenly flames spewed out of the machine. The torch blasted into the line of machines on the opposite side of the crater. They erupted in flames, and a group of them charged at me.

The *other* directed my mind to my left hand, then to darkness. The machine's arm pointed into the air and fired out a thin, black stream. Far above, the stream sprang open like a net. It blocked out the sky and dripped down, like water poured over a clear glass ball. As everything around me went pitch black, my eyes adjusted. *The machine's eyes*, I forced myself to remember. I watched the other charging machines trip and run into each other, as if unable to see.

I heard a roar behind me and turned back. At the lip of the crater behind me was a familiar sight. The dragon.

It roared again. As immense as I was, I still feared him. Even the *other*—whatever it was that shared my machine— seemed to tremble in the dragon's presence.

The dragon took flight, straight at me, jaws open. I ducked. The dragon's bite missed by inches, but its tail hit like a freight train. I *felt* the pain as the machine crashed to its side. The dragon sat back on its haunches and sneered at me. Then the dragon grew. It doubled in size. And doubled again.

I made the machine scramble away, up the side of the crater, thinking of hooks as my hands began to lose grip. Giant claws emerged and pierced into the rock wall. I climbed straight up to the crater's rim.

When I glanced back, the dragon nearly filled the whole expanse. Its head alone was larger than my giant robot. It was still growing. I felt like the earth compared to the sun. I had no chance. The dragon's jaws opened wide as if to swallow me, but instead it spoke:

"Bow down."

Its voice was Don's. Silky, smooth, and irresistible. I bowed down, the *other* bowed down, and the machine went down with us.

Then my mind was in the pipe again, and it poured back into my body in Don's palace. I'd hardly taken a breath before I realized I was not alone.

15

A BALD MAN stood there, gazing out my window. He must have shown up while I was in the training, in the machine. I shuddered—still feeling the machine's power and seeing the dragon in my mind.

"Hello?" I managed to say.

The man turned. "It's me, Alexi." He stepped closer. "It's been a while since Greece, and since you came here. About a month now, right?"

Greece. This was Don's political adviser, the man who had shown me Babylon. I hadn't recognized him at first. His mop of dark hair was shaved clean. It looked like his whole body was shaved clean. His once hairy arms were bare. Even his eyebrows were gone. "What are you doing in my room?"

"Don sent me. I would have come sooner to welcome you, but we've been very busy with this war." He motioned to the two chairs. "Please, let's sit."

I moved numbly and sat across from him, just as I'd sat across from Bruce—who I hadn't seen since. "You've been here, in the palace?" I asked.

"Mostly. The control tower is complete now. Amazing what the machines can build in a few weeks, isn't it?"

I nodded. *Control tower*—that must be what they called the glass spire rising from the palace.

"Don't get me wrong," he added, "I'd rather be in Babylon. I'm spending more and more time there. If it weren't for these zealots, I wouldn't have to be here right now. I figure in a few days I'll get to stay there as long as I want." He ran his hands over his smooth head. "I went ahead and shaved. That's required for a longer visit."

"I talked to Beatriz," I said. "She made it sound like she was going to stay in the real world."

"Oh, she and I can go back and forth, but why wouldn't I enjoy Babylon?" His eyes grew distant, then they focused on me again. "You've tasted it. Can you think of a single desire, a single sensation that the place can't satisfy?"

The memory was rich and haunting. He was right, but so, so wrong. Babylon stole souls, made people slaves. I met Alexi's eyes. "I want more out of life than sensations."

"Don't we all!" he laughed. "You just need to spend a little more time there. You'll get everything out of life you can imagine."

"What if I want hair?"

Alexi's eyes tightened for an instant, then his grin was back. "Of all people, Eli, I figured you wouldn't get caught up on the physical world. We know about your dreams. Mind over matter, right?" He looked around the room. "In here you're bound by walls and reality. Don't worry, once we win this war, you'll have a chance to revisit. You can have whatever hair you want. You have no idea how *sweet* my Babylon is . . ."

The fanatic look in his eyes made me press back into my chair. Did he really believe life was better floating like bald bacteria in amniotic fluid? "None of this explains why you're here."

"I'm here because this war's not over. Don still calls on me to help. And on you. This might be finished even sooner now that you've finally joined us. That was very impressive, what you did with the machine."

I failed to hide my surprise.

"Oh yes," he said. "I saw you."

"Have you been in one?"

"Of course," he said. "Well, one almost that strong. Don doesn't let just anyone into his masterpieces."

"How do they work? I mean, I know it's through a sync, but stronger than other drones. Sometimes I felt like I was sharing the controls."

"It's just the machine's code." Alexi leaned forward and continued in a quiet voice. "Between us, I'll admit, I don't quite understand how it works. Don keeps some of his programming separate from even me. But here's what I think. It's some master algorithm. It's almost *super*intelligent."

"You mean the machine has a mind of its own?"

"Something like that." He leaned back in the chair and laughed. "Who else is going to run things once we're all in Babylon?"

"I don't know." And I didn't want to find out. "Why does he need your help now when he's got the machines?"

"The machines still need a human mind to reach their fullest potential. And now that you've done Beatriz's training, I think you won't need much convincing. One taste of that power and you're hooked, right?"

"It's a powerful machine."

Alexi laughed. "Never easily impressed, are you? That must be why Don tolerates your messy background, your strange beliefs. You still keep a level head. You'll do well in the battle. And once we take care of the Mahdi, this should all be over. His men still fight, many of them in Jerusalem, but you know the saying: cut off the head of the snake . . ."

I kept my face blank. "The Mahdi's the only resistance left?"

"Pretty much. A few sheepherders here and there. The Amish. Isolated African tribes. No real risks."

"No countries?"

"Nope. Remember, we already took care of the politics."

I thought of the meeting of world leaders in Geneva and how they'd agreed to give Don authority, just before the Mahdi attacked. "What if the politics change? What if there's a new U.S. President who backs out of the UN?"

"Man, you've been living under a rock. When's the last time you connected your precept?"

"Earlier today."

"Well, let me tell you, just a couple weeks ago, the United States tried to do just that. The President was one of the few Americans who still went back and forth from Babylon—a reward for his loyalty to Don. But I guess when he came back, he started to regret the deal or something. Maybe he missed the power. Whatever the reason, he tried to launch an attack."

"Where?"

"Here! Can you believe that? It was an assassination attempt, pure and simple. A few thousand men and drones—some rogue holdout group of the ISA and a bunch of ex-Marines. They stormed the palace, climbing the Masada hillside like the Roman soldiers a couple thousand years ago."

"I didn't hear anything. What happened?"

Alexi smiled. "There wasn't much to hear. We killed them in a flash. Literally. Don's been experimenting for a while with electromagnetic pulses. He used one to blast the whole area around the palace. Everything within five miles was hit, but everything within our walls was safe. All the attackers went down. Weapons, too. Don ordered the drones to go out and dispatch them."

My mouth had fallen open. Don was winning every battle.

"Scary to think people would be so stupid as to attack

Don, isn't it?" Alexi eyed me knowingly. "You can imagine what happened to the President after that."

"He was killed?"

"No, no," Alexi said. "Don wouldn't do that. He visited Washington in person. He dismantled the shield protecting the city. He had the weapons ready to destroy it, and he explained this to the President, broadcasting it to everyone who wasn't already in Babylon. The President was groveling, begging for forgiveness. He apologized for America. He admitted the country had fallen from greatness, and it was only Don's and the UN's protection that sustained it. Don, of course, responded with grace. He accepted the apology, and he let the man enter Babylon, on two conditions."

"What's that?"

"One, he can never leave again. Two, everything the President sees and does in Babylon will be public. Anyone in Babylon can watch it, if they want. You could watch it even now."

"That's awful. I'll pass."

"Suit yourself. Most people aren't watching. They've got their own desires to enjoy. I know I do." He paused, licking his lips. "Any other questions? Don told me to make sure you were comfortable."

"Where's Naomi?"

"In her room." His eyes grew distant, absorbed in whatever his precept showed. "Actually, she's on her way here now. I better go." Alexi stood, and so did I.

"Why can't she sync with one of the machines? She's

just as capable as I am, if not more."

"Don has given her a different role." Alexi seemed to be choosing his words carefully. "I told you, he doesn't trust just anyone in his machines."

But I knew he didn't trust me. Alexi had made his way to the door. "Why are you going?"

"I came to answer your questions, and I've done that. Now the battle calls. You'll be joining soon." He opened the door. "Good seeing you. If you have more questions just send me a message."

I nodded as he walked out.

NAOMI CAME INTO my room without knocking, wearing the baby in a cocoon of cloth wrapped around her torso. The boy was quiet, peering up at her. He seemed too sentient for an infant. I half expected him to say something. Nothing related to Don could surprise me anymore.

"Sorry it took so long," she said. "Ready to find Ronaldo?"

"How long were you gone?"

She stepped closer. "About an hour. Why? What's wrong? Your eyes, they look different. Darker."

"I did the training, and then Alexi showed up."

"Who's that?"

"He's one of Don's closest advisors. I met him before

in Geneva. Smart guy, but weird. He's always excited about politics and the next big thing. He seems oblivious to what Don is really doing."

"Most people are." Naomi walked past me to the balcony outside, and I followed. The fresh air was nice. "What about the training?" she asked.

"Don's machines are amazing. Total vehicles of destruction."

"We already knew that."

"No, we saw it. It's different being inside one of them. You remember from ISA-7 what it's like being synced with little drones?"

She nodded.

"Well, I feel like syncing with those drones took up about 10% of my brain. This machine took up all of me . . . and more."

"You sound shaken."

"I think there was something else synced in the machine with me."

"Another person?"

"No, but kind of like that. Alexi guessed it was machine superintelligence. I doubt that. It was powerful, and it seemed to have personality. Together we could handle the machine. The other presence guided me. We crushed an army of robots. We sliced steel towers in half. But we still couldn't hold up against the dragon."

"The dragon?" she asked. "Some *other presence*?"

"Yeah, what?"

She put her hands on either side of my head and stared

into my eyes. I could see the amber flecks in her green irises.

"You can't let Don meddle with you like that. It could have been a demon. What if you were possessed?"

"I know it sounds crazy. But I wasn't possessed. Maybe Alexi was on the right track—Don could have coded some of his thinking into the machine."

She stepped back, hand on her hip, not buying it. I wasn't sure if the baby at her chest made her look more or less intimidating.

"Seriously," I said. "I feel totally fine."

"Feelings are deceptive. Is your precept off now?"

I shook my head. "V, shut down." The world went bland, but it did feel cleaner. "Happy?"

"No. Not at all. We shouldn't have tried this. Don't do it again unless we have another sign, some clear instruction, okay?"

"Okay." Maybe she was right. Maybe not.

"Come on, let's go find Ronaldo."

We ventured down the long hall with black marble floors, walls of glass, and motionless androids lining the way. The windows to our right showed the palace's courtyards. The windows to the north revealed a steep drop-off and a vast turquoise sea. Naomi's gaze stayed out over the water for most of the walk.

"I know where we are," she eventually said.

"Don called it Masada. That's the Dead Sea, right?"

She nodded. "We're not far from Jerusalem. Someone should be able to find us here."

"Ronaldo already did. That doesn't seem to have helped."

"We'll see. He may still be more help than you think. Did he give you any hints about where he is?"

We had just turned the corner to the east wing. This hallway looked more middle eastern, with sandstone walls, ornate rugs, and arched windows. There were dozens of doors, and stairs going up and down.

"He just said he was locked up in the east wing."

"Up it is."

"It's just a saying—locked *up*."

"You underestimate Ronaldo." She headed to a flight of narrow stairs at the end of the hall. The androids watched us. They always watched.

After three flights of stairs, we reached the top floor. We were breathing heavily.

"Feeling okay?" I asked.

She nodded. "I'm fine. A little tired." She glanced down. "Our walk rocked baby boy to sleep."

"I tried these stairs before, and the androids stopped me. It's weird they let us pass—like they wanted us to come up here." I eyed the hall before us nervously. "Something feels different."

"I sense it, too. But not in a bad way. I almost feel lighter here. Tell me if you see anything."

We began walking forward. The hall looked more like a prison than anything I'd seen in the palace. There weren't iron bars or guards, but there also weren't windows or decorations. Solid metal doors lined the walls, only a few paces apart.

We'd almost reached the end with no sign of Ronaldo. "How are we supposed to know where he is?" I asked.

"You sure there was no trace from his message?"

"No, nothing."

"I felt my hopes rising as we walked. I'm not afraid here." She began walking back the other way. "Ronaldo!" she called out. "Ronaldo!"

"You really think—" The sound of sliding metal interrupted me. To our left, a thin sliver of metal had opened on one of the doors. A pair of stunning, bright eyes stared out and met mine. My knees suddenly felt weak.

It wasn't Ronaldo. Ronaldo didn't have yellow halos in his eyes.

"Ronaldo!" Naomi shouted up ahead.

I heard metal sliding again. I kept my eyes on Naomi. "They're watching us."

She stopped and turned to me. "Who?"

I nodded to the door where the yellow eyes had appeared. It was solid metal again.

"Did you see something?" Naomi asked.

"Yeah, eyes."

"Whose?"

"I don't know. They didn't look human."

She wrapped her arms over the baby. "Let's find Ronaldo and get out of here."

"Good idea, but don't—"

"Ronaldo!" she called out again, pacing faster. "Ronaldo, Ronaldo, Ronaldo!"

Metal was sliding open. I felt dozens of eyes following us. I glanced to my right. Eyes like fire. To my left, irises like molten gold.

I caught up to Naomi's side and grabbed her arm. My hand was shaking. "You have to stop."

The baby's eyes opened. He stared at me like he knew me, like he understood. Then he turned his head to the side. I followed his gaze to another door, and it was opening.

17

A GIANT OF a man stood in the doorway. He had a shaved head and scars on his face. He looked us up and down, then grunted, "Who are you?"

He looked threatening, but at least he had no shadows dancing around him. I put on a confident smile. "We are the guests of President Cristo. He sent us here to talk to a man named Ronaldo."

The man scratched his head. "I doubt that. If Alexi let you up here, he must want me to take care of you."

"No, I—"

My voice caught as he pulled a gun and pointed it in my face. "Boss prefers folks alive. But he's a good boss. Gives me discretion."

Naomi stepped forward. "*How. Dare. You.*" Her voice

dripped with arrogance. "You treat the mother of the President's son like this?" She raised her hand and pointed into his face like an indignant queen. "And *you* would make *me* speak to you directly?"

She turned slightly, allowing a clear view of her son. I imagined the baby's big eyes were staring into the man's.

"No, ma'am, I mean," the man fumbled. "I'd heard about you, but—" he bowed to a knee. "It's an honor."

"The President insists that I speak to this man Ronaldo," Naomi said with contempt. "Take me to him."

"I guess that's alright. If it's important, you'll be watched anyway." The man rose up and lumbered a few steps, to the door directly across the hall. He paused. "Mr. President had me rough him up. That's what I do, ya know. Ain't no machine can scare a man like me."

"He better be hurting," Naomi said. "You know what this man did?"

The giant nodded slowly. "He's one of them religious types. Maybe even one of their leaders. I hear we got all but three now. I killed one myself."

Naomi's poker face held. "Well done."

A memory fell into place. A hulking frame standing over Jacques. "Did I hear right that you killed the Frenchman?"

The man grinned. "That one was tough to crack."

"So I hear," Naomi said, her voice tight. She pointed to Ronaldo's door. "What have you squeezed out of this man so far?"

"Oh, I'm just getting started. But he'll talk. Don't

worry."

"I never worry," Naomi said. "We'll see what we can learn first."

The man nodded and pulled the door open. Naomi glided past without giving him another glance. I followed after her into a the thin corridor. Each step made me feel like I was being squeezed tighter in a vice. The tight hall opened onto a dark, bare room. Its only light was from a small holograph of Don's face in a corner. His eyes stared down at us.

"Naomi!" Ronaldo rose to his bare feet. Chains connected the shackles at his wrists to the floor. He looked down at the baby. "Ya boy's beautiful!"

"Thank you," she said, concern thick in her voice. "It's good to see you alive."

"Just a matter of days." Ronaldo dipped his head. As Naomi stepped to the side, I saw the bruises and bloody marks on his face. His nose bent sharply to the side.

"Elijah! Good to see ya, mon."

I stepped closer and I embraced him, gently. "You too," I said, "but I'm sorry to see you in here."

"It's no matter. My soul is free. My God is with me. What more could a man want?"

I smiled. No one could keep this man down. "Maybe some privacy." I motioned to the holograph of Don. "I assume that's just a recording?"

"Mon, assume nothin' about the devil. This is his domain. He watchin' us, but that don't bother me, because the Lord is watchin' too."

"We came as soon as we got your message," Naomi said.

"I barely got it off before an android caught me. Now I can't send a bit of data through these doors. But there's plenty to keep me busy."

"Like what?" I asked.

"Ya think I don't have anything to pray about? This ain't no tropical vacation."

I suddenly remembered the eyes I'd seen peering through the doors. "Did you see anything strange when you were brought here? Whatever's in the other cells heard Naomi when she was calling for you."

Ronaldo shook his head. "What did ya see?"

"Eyes. They were like fire. Yellow and gold."

Ronaldo and Naomi exchanged a look. "Angels?" Ronaldo asked.

"Maybe, but I've seen an angel," I said, thinking of Michael hammering a hole through rock. "No way they could be kept locked up like this. They're too strong."

"This is the devil's prison, mon." He looked to Naomi. "What do we know about angels being held up?"

"It's happened before," she said. "The angel who visited Daniel told him *the prince of the kingdom of Persia withstood me twenty-one days*. But Michael helped him get out."

"Then Michael will help again." Ronaldo sounded certain. "Let's make the most of this place until then. What can I do for you now?"

"Shouldn't we be asking you that?" I said.

"Sure should," he said, "it's a question we should

always be askin' others. But even a jailed man can pray."

"We have a lot of questions," Naomi said.

"Let's hear 'em." Ronaldo motioned for us to sit. The shackles at his wrists slid slightly, revealing bloody sores underneath.

We sat on the hard floor across from him. "For starters," Naomi said, "what's going on outside the palace walls? We've had no safe way to get information."

"It's not good," Ronaldo said. "We lost Neo. Don's huntin' down anyone who didn't go to Babylon. Some of them are believers, but some were just too old or too poor to have precepts. If they'll take a precept after they're caught, then Don lets them go to Babylon. If not . . . well, we don't know, we've never seen one of them again."

"He's a murderer." Naomi stared down at her baby, shaking her head slowly.

"It's only going to get worse before the Lord comes."

"So what's next?" I asked.

"If *you* don't know," Ronaldo said, "then none of us know. Concerning that day and hour no one knows, not even the angels of heaven, nor the Son, but the Father only."

"That's from the Bible?"

Ronaldo nodded. "And here's another one: the Lord will be revealed from heaven with his mighty angels in flaming fire, inflicting vengeance on those who do not know God and on those who do not obey the gospel of our Lord Jesus."

"Sounds pretty harsh," I said.

"Is it harsh if it's just?" Naomi replied.

"Not if God's dealin' the justice," Ronaldo said. "Like always, there's no use guessin' about the time. What matters is what we do now. We gotta testify. We gotta pray. We gotta fight for Him."

I remembered my training and Don's offer. "Don wants me to sync with one of his machines and fight in the battle against the Mahdi. Why do you think he wants that, and should I do it?"

Ronaldo was quiet before answering. "God gave ya a gift, Elijah. I told ya before, ain't nothin' the devil wants more than to twist God's plan. That means he'll do anything, *anything*, to make God's gifts his own. The more special the gift, the more desperate he'll be to steal it."

"But he knows Elijah is on our side now," Naomi said.

"Nah." Ronaldo shook his head, dreadlocks swinging. "It ain't that simple. Just 'cuz he knows Elijah joined us don't mean it's finished. This battle for souls goes to the last day. Ya know the story of the wheat and the weeds?"

"No," I said.

Ronaldo smiled. "Listen, Jesus said the kingdom of heaven is like a man who planted good seed in his field, but while his men were sleeping, his enemy came and planted weeds among the wheat and went away. So when the plants grew, the weeds grew too. The master told his servants to let both grow together until the harvest, and at harvest time he'd tell the reapers: *gather the weeds first and bind them in bundles to be burned, but gather the wheat into my barn.* Ya get that?"

"I think so," I said. "The enemy is the devil?"

"Sure is. The harvest is comin' any day now. I figure the reapers are God's angels. The weeds are whoever goes to the evil one. So maybe you're wheat, Elijah, but the devil wants ya to be a weed. We can't know for sure until the harvest."

"This has to be a trap," Naomi said. "It makes no sense for Elijah to waltz into it and sync with Don's machine."

"I ain't so sure. The devil sets traps everywhere he goes, but he controls only as much as God lets him. Maybe there's a trap within a trap. What the devil seeks for evil, God can use for good. Elijah, what ya seen or heard from the Lord?"

The words I remembered calmed my feverish mind. "You know what I heard before Don caught us, right? About speaking to the world."

Ronaldo nodded.

"The only thing since then is that I should *trust and wait*. And I keep having dreams about my Mom taking me to the dragon in Jerusalem and about a huge, blazing fire coming to burn up the world."

"Hmm, trust and wait." Ronaldo leaned forward and rested his shackled hands on his knees. "Ya better get comfortable. You're reborn, Elijah, but as newborn as this baby." He motioned to Naomi's son, still sleeping soundly. "We drink milk before we're ready for the real food of the spirit. We gonna wait here as long as it takes. Let's pray."

Naomi put her hand on my knee and met my eyes. "Jesus said, where two or three are gathered in my name, there I am with them."

"Even in a prison cell?" I said. "Shouldn't we try to get you out of these chains?"

Ronaldo shook his head. "We gotta pray. Ready?"

Naomi nodded and closed her eyes. I did the same.

"Lord Jesus Christ," Ronaldo began, speaking with a slow cadence, "we gather in your name, seeking ya even here, in the enemy's home. Only your light can pierce darkness this thick. Be with us, speak to us. Lord, we listenin' . . . ."

His voice trailed off and left the sound of silence. I listened carefully, grasping for hope that I'd hear something. I could hear Ronaldo and Naomi and the baby breathing. I could hear my own deep breaths. That was it. Time ticked by like water from a slowly dripping faucet.

After a while, Ronaldo started murmuring something under this breath. I couldn't make out the words, but he sounded intense. I adjusted my weight, trying to get comfortable on the hard ground.

Then I heard the sound of sliding metal.

18

DON WAS STRIDING in, looking everything like a president and nothing like a devil. "I see you've found each other." He leaned against the prison cell's wall.

Ronaldo surged to his feet, but Don silenced us with a raised hand. "The battle is going well. The Muslims have their backs against the wall in Tehran. We surround the city. The Mahdi's last stand will be any day now, and what a last stand! These people truly believe they can defeat me. They won't surrender. Every last one of them will die." Don straightened his tie casually. "Eli, you passed your training. Well done. You will join me tomorrow."

"He's not your pawn," Naomi said.

Don's gaze swiveled to her. "The mother of my son speaks." She squirmed under his stare. Her face went pale, lips pressed together in a thin line.

"But of course," Don continued, shifting his eyes back to me, "why would I force anything? The Muslims will try to kill us, but I'm giving Eli my very best weapon."

A chill went down my spine as I remembered the other presence that had operated the drone with me. "It was quite a machine," I said. "I'm surprised I could control it."

"It takes more than a gifted mind," he said. "This is beyond what is seen. My power knows no limits."

"You lie, Satan!" Ronaldo's words burst out like water from a dam. "You get only what God lets ya have. Ya reign is short, evil, and dyin'. Ya gonna lose, gonna burn!"

"You finished?" Don picked at his nails.

"I'm just warmin' up. I rebuke you, in the name of Jesus Christ. Get back, Satan!" Ronaldo moved toward him. "I say, in the name of—"

Don held up his hand and Ronaldo stopped, as if the words were strangled in his throat. "That's enough. I prefer not to hear that name in *MY kingdom*. Understood?"

Ronaldo stared him down, but fear was in his eyes. "What did I tell ya?" he growled. "Ain't no corruption like power on this earth."

"Corruption?" Don laughed. "Is that what you call change, growing toward freedom? Then yes, I suppose I do corrupt little slaves into fuller pleasure." He turned to me. "I tire of this. It's getting late, and you must prepare to fight by my side tomorrow."

"What if he doesn't?" Naomi's voice was soft. Her gaze was fixed on the baby at her chest. "Do you need him so that you can be exalted? Or is it just spite?"

Don's smile wavered. "I will be exalted for what I give the people. Eli can either enjoy the honor by my side or share the fate of Ronaldo and the rest of the order."

"And my fate?" Naomi looked up slowly and met Don's gaze.

"That depends. If Eli joins me, he saves you. Otherwise, yes . . . you'll die like the rest of them." Don glanced at Ronaldo as if he were a stray dog. "Like the Brazilian."

All their eyes settled on me. Joining meant wielding immense power. It meant getting out of this palace. It meant opportunity. Not joining meant doing nothing, hiding in fear, but did it also mean trusting and waiting on God? *Do I let Naomi die or deal with the devil?*

Don's hand reached out toward me.

I couldn't let Naomi die, not like this. I'd trade my life for hers.

Trust. I clasped his hand.

Don smiled and shook it firmly. I felt as if power were entering me.

"You will *not* harm Elijah." Naomi looked down as the baby began to make waking noises. "Remember, the fate of your son depends on me."

Don released my hand and turned to her. "Sometimes I forget how young you are, and how little you know." He put one hand on her cheek, and the other on the baby's head. "Such misplaced faith makes my victory all the sweeter." He smiled, exultant. "There's no finer taste than the blood of martyrs."

The way he looked at her made me cringe. "Stop touching her."

Don stepped back and grinned at me. "As you wish. She's my gift to you, after all. Come." He motioned for Naomi and me to follow. "Ronaldo has a date with my little helper, who you've now met. Androids will escort you back to your quarters."

19

BIRDS SANG OVERHEAD as I walked through the rainforest. My hands grazed over green plants with soft and silky leaves. A fresh breeze blew against my bare skin. I breathed in deeply. The smell was decadent and tropical. I caught hints of every fruit I could imagine—pineapples, mangos, kiwis. The trees rose high as skyscrapers above me.

I came to a river of dark blue, peaceful water. A woman was swimming along with the current. Our eyes met.

"Come in!" she said, waving and laughing. "It's wonderful."

I waded into the cool water. I gasped as it touched my stomach, then I dove fully under. I sprang off the river's bottom and my head splashed out. I shouted to the sky.

The woman laughed with me as we swam easily toward each other. She took my hands in hers. "Let's go to the island and let the sun warm us dry."

I nodded. We swam together to an island in the middle of the river. It was not far, but my breath was rushed, exhilarated as we stepped onto the island's shore.

"There." The woman pointed to a large flat stone that stuck out over the river. Droplets of water fell from her outstretched arm, from her hair, down her chest and legs. We wore only our skin, and neither of us seemed to notice. We lay on our backs on the stone. I closed my eyes and felt my body's weight settle against the smooth, warm surface. The sun played on my eyelids. It dried my skin. I fell into sleep within sleep.

"Let's go." The woman was tapping my shoulder. I opened my eyes. The sun was like a halo over her head. "You hungry?"

I nodded and stood.

She laughed and pulled me along by the hand. We came to the only tree on the island. It was in the center, with a trunk wider than I was tall. Its branches arched and swooped low to the ground around us. Looking up through its gnarled wood, bending and turning, dividing and reaching, I had a sense of great age, as if this tree had been here before the forest, the river, and even the earth. I was a newborn before an ancient.

"Here." The woman held out a bright red fruit.

I took it in my hand. It fit easily in my palm, but was heavy as a stone. "We don't eat this," I said.

Her lips curled up at the ends, luscious and happy. "He said the taste is good, so good we'll never forget it. Let's just try it."

"Who said that?"

"Him." She pointed to one of the tree's low branches, which bent all the way to the ground. There, wound around the wood, watching us, was a serpent.

"Do I know you?" I asked.

The creature's slitted eyes blinked closed then open, and so did mine. Only, when mine opened, the tree and everything else were gone. I sat up and rubbed my eyes.

An android stood beside my bed, sending a shiver down my spine. I had no idea how long it had been there.

Its machine arms held out some clothes. "Get dressed. Time to go."

"Where?"

"Don is waiting. The battle begins soon."

I rose from my bed, still disoriented. I barely remembered falling asleep after an android had escorted me back to my room the night before. Sleep had brought the dream, and the dream had brought that alluring vision.

I took the suit, black as usual. The android waited at the door for me to put it on. I had a feeling this was my last chance to back out. I thought of Ronaldo, locked up in prison. My stomach growled, reminding me of Ronaldo's words. Real food of the spirit. I needed that. I needed to pray.

God, do I go?

I waited. I buttoned my shirt.

Why would you let the devil give me this choice? Naomi might die if I don't go.

I finished buttoning. My fingers were tying the tie when a verse came to me, clear as day. It was something I'd read, maybe back on the boat with Ronaldo. Now it rang true: *Do not fear what you are about to suffer . . . Be faithful unto death, and I will give you the crown of life.*

Faithful unto death. Trust and wait. Would this give me a chance to speak for the Lord? I could certainly reach more people if I weren't trapped in the palace, and it was my chance to save Naomi. I had to go. And so I did.

The android led me out. We walked from the palace's west wing to one of the inner areas. We eventually passed through a door that had always been locked for me. We came to a room that looked like a wheel's hub. It had hallways leading six different directions. In the center of the room was a glass column.

An elevator rose up before us a moment later, the doors sliding open and the android stepping in. I entered and we shot up. The elevator took us outside as if we were flying through the glass spire that loomed over the palace. I gazed out over the Dead Sea and desert hills beyond. I looked up and saw a disc shape—the control tower, Alexi had said. The elevator stopped inside the disc and I stepped out.

I was in a round operations center. The window panels were screens encircling the room. The floor and ceiling were bright, polished white. I counted ten white chairs in a circle facing out toward the screens. The men and women sitting in the chairs were wearing wired helmets over their heads. None of them turned as I entered. I saw only their backs.

One chair was empty.

I glanced back and saw the elevator descend again. The glass column lowered until it was flush with the floor. And there, in the heart of the room, in the center of the white chairs, was a large crimson chair with arms coiled like serpents. Don sat there, watching me.

"Welcome to the war," he said. "Take your seat."

20

AS I MOVED to the open seat, I saw faces I recognized. Alexi. Beatriz. Two from the gathering of the world's richest in Geneva—Xing Xing and the young guy from India. I did not know the other four. Everyone's eyes were closed, their faces focused. Synced.

Don came to my side. "Sit."

I sat. As soon as I did, the helmet lowered over my head. Its translucent wires prodded like little parasitic worms seeking a point of entry.

"You will have the machine you trained in," Don said, "but first you will receive a briefing of the battlefield. Heed every detail. The Persians want to kill you. Kill them first. See you in Tehran." He spun away.

My precept came on without request. The sync took

over. My body was in Don's control tower, but my mind was transported a million miles away.

A map of the world filled my vision. Almost every spot of land had a layer of crimson covering it, as if painted in blood. The color was thicker and darker in places. But in a few tiny dots, the reddish tint grew so faint that there was white. Was that the resistance? The order? The dots were few and far between. They looked splattered from the fling of a painter's brush. A handful in America, China. A few more in Africa.

The view began zooming in on the Middle East. A green expanse filled the center of the area, dark as an emerald around the region, but lighter as it merged into red on the edges. That had to be the Muslim resistance. The Mahdi's people. The area around Jerusalem was splattered in red, green, white, and even a couple specks of blue. Jewish people, I guessed. My people.

Some days ago, on November 19, said Beatriz's voice in my mind, *the resistance began Ramadan, and we launched our reclamation project.*

The colors on the map began to shift. Lines of red plunged into the green, piercing like arrows from the north, east, south, and west. Each arrow plunged farther and expanded. Red swept over the Arabian peninsula. Red from the north and south met and swallowed every trace of green down the middle of the region. Red from the west dripped down over North Africa; it bent around Jerusalem and flooded east, turning a rich crimson color with no specks of white. A circle of green remained farther east, darkest around Tehran. I imagined Aisha and the Mahdi there, holding against Don's forces.

Beatriz's voice came again. *As of yesterday, December 7, nearly all the resistance had accepted our offer of peace. They laid down their arms, exalted Don, and entered Babylon. Two cities remain. We have already established our stronghold near Jerusalem. Don will take it last. Today we send all our forces to Tehran, to finish the enemy.*

My view suddenly panned to the other side of the world. It zoomed onto a large island in the Pacific, onto a dense range of mountains, onto an immense crater. A mine cut deep into the earth.

Don awaits you, Beatriz said. *He will lead the attack from above. I expect you'll be at his side. Follow his commands to the letter, or Naomi dies.*

And then I was in the machine, my senses reeling. This crater was the same place as the training. The *other* something was sharing the controls, channeling my thoughts away from Naomi, away from the past, and toward what was facing us: the dragon.

The black creature stood on its hind legs with wings spreading across the crater. Its jaws snapped open and unleashed a roar that sent stones tumbling down the crater's sides. But as the roar hit me, words came into my mind: *You understand me?*

I nodded. I felt like the *other* was grinning. If the machine could have grinned, it would have too.

What is in this machine? I asked in my head.

The dragon leapt off the ground and roared again. *Your*

partner. Azazel. With a flick of his wings, the dragon soared up into the sky. *Follow.*

Azazel? Who was that? And how was I supposed to fly? As if answering all my thoughts, the *other*, this *Azazel*, directed my mind to my back. The option to fly appeared. We chose it, and we set our tracker on the dragon and flew straight up like a missile.

What are you? I asked.

No answer. I looked down. The earth was far away, and our trajectory flattened, almost like reaching orbit. My mind felt out of control as it went to the machine's core. Options appeared: diagnostics, usage, shield, and charge. I chose diagnostics. Then, in the machine's view, my view, a screen flashed. It showed a hundred numbers, impossible to parse at once. In the center were two names with percentages.

Elijah: 50%.

Azazal: 50%.

I tried to make sense of it. We shared the machine, but I felt like I barely had control. Azazel's presence was like a shadow, hard to see, impossible to grasp.

The dragon roared up ahead. The sound washed over me, and again I understood it. *Destroy everything. Leave the Mahdi to me.*

We dove toward the earth like two crashing meteors. The machine's enhanced vision revealed the terrain below, and the targets. We were heading straight for Tehran, the sprawling city wedged against a wall of mountains. Fires burned throughout. Columns of black smoke billowed into the smoggy sky. Don's other machines were advancing from all angles, except from above. That was us.

Just as I could make out armored soldiers manning rockets below, a cloud of blackness spewed out of the dragon's mouth. Its roar pulsed in violent waves like a sonic attack. Surely every person within miles could hear it. The sound became words of raw, gut-curling hate in my mind: *Follow, detonate, BURN.*

The dragon landed atop an immense building. My machine's feet came down beside it. The building stood on two outspread legs in the center of a vast grassy area. The machine was almost as tall as the building, and the masses of soldiers gathered around like armored ants.

As they opened fire, the dragon lifted his head in the sky and roared: *Dig.*

Again Azazel took control. The machine leapt off the building to the ground. I could *feel* the crunch of men beneath me. Their missiles were gnats buzzing around. The machine's legs sprang into my mind, followed by options. One was dig, and suddenly the legs shifted and combined and transformed into an enormous drill. It bored into the ground, throwing dirt. The machine's head dipped below the earth. I could see nothing but brown.

In moments, the ground below gave out and the machine dropped. I landed with a hard crash of metal, but the machine sprang back to its feet, rising in an immense cavern of gleaming metal and blinking lights. A group was facing me. Maybe a hundred soldiers, their faces shocked, their guns raised.

A man in the center—the Mahdi—began to shout in Farsi. V translated: "Hold fire. It's useless. If the drone attacks, we detonate. Pray to Allah."

Detonate? I scanned the cavern and understood immediately. Dozens of missiles were clustered in the center of the room. Each bore the familiar symbol of a black and yellow wheel. This was a nuclear silo.

Steady now. It was Azazel's thought. He was speaking to me.

Probabilities appeared on a screen overlaying the machine's vision. They showed a 0.07% chance that we'd kill all these men before they could detonate the missiles, unless the machine unleashed so much firepower that it set off the missiles here and now.

I tried to force my mind away from the machine, away from Azazel. I tried to pray. *God! Help me! What do you want?*

WAIT, came His voice.

Wait? Again? I scanned the room, confused. I noticed a smaller, cloaked figure behind the Mahdi. A woman. *Wait.*

Azazel shoved the thought away. He directed me to the machine's wrists. An array of attack options appeared. I summoned every ounce of will to pick nothing, to wait, but it was like trying to stay motionless in a raging ocean. *Fire now*, Azazel demanded.

I fought back. *Wait.*

Fire now! Azazel pressed harder. I resisted. I did nothing. The machine did nothing. *Fire or we kill Naomi.*

NO, I thought. *Wait.*

The group of Persians began to stir. The woman came

to the Mahdi's side and whispered into his ear. Then she turned to me. I knew her almond eyes. It was Aisha.

21

I TRIED TO make the machine speak: *Aisha*. But no noise came as she stared at me. She saw only a metal behemoth.

Azazel's will slammed into mine. He wouldn't let the machine talk. I wouldn't let it attack. He was rage and fury. I was trust and wait. Stalemate.

Aisha whispered again into the Mahdi's ear. He looked hesitant but nodded to whatever she'd said. He issued a command that rang out in the cavern. V translated: "Return to your stations."

The men scattered around the room. Most of them sat in chairs like mine in Don's control tower, with syncing helmets covering their heads. They were probably in battle above ground.

I kept the machine's eyes on Aisha while holding my

resistance against Azazel. She approached a table and began gathering up small metallic objects. I zoomed the machine's view—she had collected a bundle of bug-like trackers. She placed a circuit board on the side of her head, like the Captain's except over her dark hair, and she stepped toward my machine.

The Mahdi took her arm gently, and they embraced. When she turned back to me, her face was pure resolve. Her stride lengthened into a run as she came at the machine.

She reached the machine's enormous feet, barely as tall as its ankles. She started climbing up like a spider.

Ankle, Azazel demanded. *Fire!*

I fought for stillness in my mind. I watched Aisha rise up the machine's metal frame, while Azazel shouted inside it, inside *me*: *Kill her! Fire!* I was a cracking dam against the flood of his rage, but I managed to hold—barely.

Aisha reached the machine's head. She hung before its camera-eyes, peering into them. With one hand clasped to the visor above those eyes, she used her other hand to place the little metal bugs directly on the machine.

She's hacking me. It was brilliant. She was going to try to code her way into the machine. The same way I'd hacked into the android in Alexi's palace. Azazel jerked my mind to different parts of the machine, but my vision filled with the universe eyes from my dream. Those eyes from the throne—stillness and judgment and power—they held me, wouldn't let me cave, wouldn't let the machine budge.

Aisha had pulled herself up to the top of the machine's

head as the bugs began scurrying like ants over the surface. Alarms rang out in my mind as the bugs began to burrow into seams of metal, as a foreign code entered into the machine's operating system.

Then Aisha entered, body and mind. She'd climbed inside.

Elijah!? Aisha thought in shock. *You're in here? And what—who is sharing the controls?*

It's me. And one of Don's servants, named Azazel. He's powerful.

Azazel. A demon's name, Aisha thought. *The two of us have to take control. We have to get out. NOW. I'll try to resist Azazel. You make us fly.*

Done. I thought of the machine's back. I felt Azazel resisting me, but Aisha was right. The two of us, working together, could contain him. I made the option appear: fly. I selected it and the rumble of the machine's jets filled the cavern.

I looked up just before we lifted off the ground. The tunnel to the earth's surface was blocked by machines swarming down. They flooded into the cavern and left no way out . . . unless I attacked.

I'd waited this long. I waited again. *We wait*, I shared with Aisha.

For now, she agreed.

"Well done!" shouted Don, yanking my gaze back into the cavern. He was there in the body, walking out of one of the machines that had just landed. His eyes passed over my machine, and he nodded as if in thanks. He walked on toward the Mahdi and his men. With six giant killing machines at his back, Don could demolish these men. But he was there, in the open, unarmed, walking toward their raised guns. Could they kill him? A single shot? A nuclear suicide?

Don's casual stride paraded contempt. "The time has finally come," he said to the Mahdi, his voice echoing off the metallic walls. "Lay down your arms, bow down to me, and you may live."

The Mahdi spoke solemnly, and V translated, *"There is no deity but Allah."* He continued in English. "It was never supposed to go this far. Take another step, Dajjal, and none of us will leave this bunker alive."

Don stopped in front of the Mahdi. "You cannot kill me, but I welcome the effort. I always wondered whether you would be used as friend or foe. Go ahead and destroy. Be my friend."

"You lie, Dajjal."

"Sometimes," Don shrugged, "but not this time. Do you see me trying to stop you?"

"It would be better for the world to die than for you to reign over it." The Mahdi raised his arm, aiming a gun at Don. "Best of all would be you dying. Any last words?"

"You should know that you have been all I wanted you to be." Don's voice was sincere, exultant.

Then the Mahdi pulled the trigger. Nothing happened.

He pulled it again. Nothing.

"What?" he stammered. "What are you doing?"

Don reached forward, and the Mahdi just stood there

in shock as Don took the gun. "Let me try."

He aimed at the head of a man just behind the Mahdi. He pulled the trigger. *BANG*.

The man collapsed. Others rushed to him, shouting.

Don watched them idly, then raised the gun again at the Mahdi. "Silence," he demanded. The men obeyed. "Last chance. Where's your faith, brother?"

The Mahdi said nothing. His bearded face was solemn.

Don leveled the gun at his head. "Any last words?"

"Shoot me and it all blows," the Mahdi whispered. "You and everything you care about." His voice rose. "Rockets in a dozen silos will launch. The lands you've taken from me will burn, from the Mediterranean Sea to the Kashmir Mountains. Your crown jewel, Jerusalem, will be a crater in the ground."

"By all means," Don taunted, "give it a try."

The Mahdi shook his head. "You will take the shot. You will bring this destruction, not me."

"This is your choice. You always knew we couldn't both rule in the end. Only I am the Morning Star. You will worship me."

"Never," the Mahdi growled. "I bear witness that there is none worthy of worship but Allah. Take the shot. Paradise awaits me, but you will burn in hell."

"Sorry my friend, but this hell is the only one you'll ever know." Don pointed the gun down and fired.

NO! Aisha gasped in my mind. The Mahdi screamed as he fell, clutching his leg.

"You will bow." Don fired again, hitting the Mahdi's

other leg.

The Mahdi writhed on the ground in pain. Men rushed to him, as he managed to lean up on an elbow.

"You will die!" he shouted. He pulled something from his cloak. "DIE AND BURN, DAJJAL!"

He fell back to the ground, but he held his arm high, device in hand. Then he pressed his thumb down.

22

"FIVE," said a voice over the intercom, filling the cavern.

Men started running. Aisha shouted in my mind, *fly!*

"FOUR."

My mind went to the machine's jets. Azazel did not resist. The machine rumbled for launch.

"THREE."

The machine took off, soaring up through the hole it had dug in the ground. As we burst out of the hole, I glimpsed a city laid waste. The other machines flew out of the hole just after mine.

TWO, I guessed. I saw a speck on the west horizon. Azazel directed my sights to it. I didn't know where to go, and in my indecision, Azazel seized the controls. We flew west like a bullet over land.

ONE, I guessed, then *BOOM!*

The explosion shook the air. Its force jerked the machine down, spinning toward the ground. As we regained balance and continued flight, I glanced back. A mushroom cloud billowed out of the earth like an erupting volcano. It swallowed what had been Tehran and everything around it.

We'd made it out.

Look! thought Aisha, frantic.

In an empty spot of desert ahead of us, a missile flew out of the ground, soaring west.

We have to stop it, I thought, locking the machine's sights on the slender rocket.

We began closing on it, but slowly. The machine was already at its fastest speed. It calculated the time before we'd catch the missile. *93 seconds*, showed the machine's screen.

Map, I commanded. *Track approach.*

A translucent map appeared before me. We were a green dot flying due west, heading straight at Jerusalem, following the red dot that was the missile just ahead. And we were too slow. The missile was going to hit the city seconds before we caught it.

Worse, other red dots were approaching from every angle. Six other green dots were in the area. Even if they were Don's other machines, it didn't seem like enough. The missiles outnumbered them four to one.

Abort! Aisha thought. *Go into orbit, or go south. We won't catch it. We have to get away.*

We can't let the city be destroyed. Naomi is in Don's palace, just outside the city. She would die. Then it hit me: my body was there, too. And Ronaldo's.

Aisha: *You know we can't stop them. And my body is in HERE! If we fly into the heart of the explosion I have no chance. Maybe Don's palace will escape the worst of it.*

She was right. I saw the Dead Sea ahead. *Trust. Wait.* Jerusalem was on the horizon. I had to save what I could. I had to trust God with the rest.

I made the machine veer hard south, aiming at the Dead Sea. Maybe the water would cushion the explosion. Maybe I could save Aisha.

Just before the machine plunged into the water, just before the missiles hit Jerusalem, just as I screamed out a last plea to God—the sky flashed.

Not a bomb. Not an explosion. Something bigger, brighter.

My mind ejected from the machine.

23

ALL SIGNS OF the machine, the Mahdi, and Aisha were gone. I was in Don's control tower again. I staggered from my chair, my head spinning. The room was bright as daylight streamed in, but everything else was dark and quiet. No lights. No technology. No friends.

"What . . . what was that?" Alexi asked from the other side of the room, rubbing his bald head, looking as confused as I felt.

"We lost our connection," Beatriz answered. "Had to be the nukes."

"No, no! Of course not," came Sven's excited voice. I'd never expected to hear the Captain's double-crossing technology agent again. "The President had anticipated all that. We were ready for the explosions."

He and the others were gathering around a hulking man before a dark control panel. I did a quick count. Eleven of us in the room, but not Don.

"Where is the President?" Alexi asked.

No one answered at first. I thought of Naomi. I checked for her through my precept, but it was gone. I had to get out. I began inching toward the center of the room, where the elevator shaft was open.

"He'll be fine," said a deep, rumbling voice. It was the man at the control panel. "The Master will bring him here. But we've lost Babylon."

"We lost all power," Sven confirmed. "Once it's back, I can reboot the system."

I crouched by the open shaft and peered down. It was like a glass tube back to earth. There was a thin ladder stretching all the way down. I slid to my stomach and swung my leg over the edge. Quietly. Carefully. If I fell, I'd die.

"This doesn't make sense," Beatriz whined. "What about our generators? We can't just lose power."

My foot found a rung of the ladder.

"Whatever happened," Sven continued, "it wiped out all our connections—to the satellites, to precepts, to people. There are no signs of electricity anywhere. It was like a giant electromagnetic bomb hit the earth."

I took a step down. My hand gripped the ladder's rail.

"He has started fighting back," said the deep-voiced man. "He used the sun."

"The sun?" Sven asked.

"What does that mean?" Beatriz sounded afraid.

I took another step down. Then another. Before ducking fully into the shaft, I glanced one last time at the control room.

The unknown man had seen me. He was staring at me, eyes slitted like the dragon's. "The last battle is here," he said, rising to his feet, stirring the shadows twisting around him. "No running now."

Everyone turned to me. The man—the demon—charged.

I gripped my hands around the cool metal rails. I pressed my feet hard against their outer edges. Then I slid as fast as I could. I kept my eyes up as I soared down, wind whipping at me through the tunnel.

Slitted eyes peered over the edge. Then the demon jumped, hurling down at me with his arms out wide, like a free diver off a cliff. There was nowhere to go. I braced for impact.

He slammed into me like a bag of bricks.

My grip gave, and I fell, with him clutching me. A rush of wind stung my face. The ground was closer and closer. Tears filled my eyes.

The demon took my chin in his hand and jerked my head to face him. His eyes were pure red, with razor-thin black slits through the middle. They were storming, swallowing me. I tried to turn my face away, but his grip was iron. I was going to die, and those terrible eyes would be the last thing I'd see. Then I remembered to close my eyes.

Thank you, God, I prayed. *It's been a good run. I go to your arms. Protect Naomi, protect—*

As I continued, I felt peace. Every fiber in me released. Then I landed. Like a feather.

The vice grip on my chin was gone. I opened my eyes. The radiant face of a woman was peering down at me. I realized I was in her arms.

Had she caught me?

"You did well, Elijah." She smiled. "I'm Laoth."

"You must go now," said a man, only his voice sounded like thunder. He was beside the woman. He was huge and armored and glowing like gold, with massive wings behind him. One of his fists clenched the demon's throat.

I knew his face. "Michael!"

He nodded. Laoth set me down on the ground. Against all odds, my knees did not buckle. I looked around me. There were dozens of them. Only Michael wore armor, but the others had the same force and light.

Angels.

A hand found mine and squeezed it. "Some of them were locked up," Naomi said, pulling me into her arms. "It's okay now. Michael came as soon as the flare hit. He broke the prison walls. Don's guards were no match, especially once the power went down."

"Flare?" I tried to make sense of it all. "What do you mean?"

"A solar flare, a flash from the sun. It slammed into earth with a huge electromagnetic pulse. It wiped out everything with electricity or a chip. Precepts, batteries, Babylon—all gone."

I could barely get my head around this. What would happen to the androids? To all the people in those capsules along the towers? I remembered the words of the demon who'd attacked me—*the Master will bring him here*. I pointed at the demon's motionless body in Michael's grip. "I don't think the power will stay off for long. He said Don will be back."

"Malphas knows nothing," Michael said. "The day of the Lord comes soon, but more still must be tested, more must be saved. We will engage Lucifer's minions until then. He will go after the child." The angel, with one hand still clamping the demon's throat, looked at the baby. Naomi wore it swaddled against her chest. "We will hold Malphas and the others here. You go now." He turned to Laoth. "Gabriel has secured the way. Take Dumah and Cassiel."

Laoth nodded and looked to Naomi and me. "Follow me."

NAOMI AND I rushed down a long hall in Don's palace. Laoth led the way, and the two other angels walked at our sides. Lifeless androids lined the walls, their big eyes almost innocent without the shadowy, blinking lights.

"What happened back there?" Naomi asked.

I kept my eyes ahead, tensed. "Don's followers were synced to giant war machines, just like the one from my training." I told her about the control tower and the bunker in Tehran, about Don and the Mahdi. "The city, the people, everything—they're gone, blown away. I couldn't stop it, couldn't even help."

"Why not?"

"It was like before. A demon shared the controls."

"I knew this was a bad idea."

"I'm still not sure." It felt like the right decision. I'd failed to save the city. I hadn't been able to fight Don because of Azazel. But now I knew about Azazel. And I had resisted him . . . with help. "I may have saved Aisha."

"She was there?"

I nodded. "With the Mahdi in the bunker. She got into my machine. Not just hacking—but with her body. She helped me resist Azazel, and—"

"Wait. Azazel?"

"Yeah. Don told me the demon's name was Azazel. I don't know how, I don't know why, but he had some control over me when I was synced with the machine."

"This way," Laoth called out. She had stopped up ahead, waiting for us. As we approached, I gazed past her and out the windows to the Dead Sea sparkling in the distance.

"Elijah is right," Laoth said, turning down another hallway. "Many of our fallen brethren have been twisted so deeply that they can never again walk on earth. Azazel is one of these. For many years Lucifer was limited in how he could use them. But through this technology, he found a new purpose for them."

"Why technology?" Naomi asked.

"There's no way around the natural laws of this planet," Laoth said. "When beings from another dimension enter here, they are bound by God's creation. Lucifer knows this. He also rebels only when he thinks he can win. He was wrong the first time, but he has learned much since then. His power is greater now than it has ever been."

"Why did he think he could win the first time?"

"Why does anyone attempt to be his own god?" Laoth sighed as she continued gliding ahead. "There is only one true cause: the pride of the created can blind them to their creator. Even after God hurled Lucifer out of heaven, the fallen angel thought he could reign secure in hell. He preferred that to serving God."

"*Better to reign in Hell, than serve in Heav'n*," Naomi recited.

I looked at her with a question in my eyes.

She shrugged. "Milton. Paradise Lost."

My faint memory of the epic poem summoned thoughts of my Adam-and-Eve dream . . . and the snake. "I'd prefer Paradise Regained."

"You've read it?" she asked.

"I started it once."

"You should finish."

I smiled. "Just waiting for the right time." I turned back to Laoth. "So Lucifer rebelled and lost. How could he be so powerful now?"

"The enemy was right in one respect," Laoth said. "He enjoyed some freedom here, and he found a way to grow in power, by feeding on men's souls. Never have so many been enslaved to him."

"What does that mean?" I asked.

"Controlling spirits requires immense force. Lucifer reigns over the fallen angels, but he cannot always control them in this realm. Now they have all been unleashed. We will fight them, but we would lose without the Lord."

"Jesus is coming again," Naomi said. "Doesn't Don know that, and that he'll lose in the end?"

"Maybe, maybe not," Laoth said. "We believe in the Word, in His promise. Lucifer does not. He's probably thinking it is uncertain whether the Lord will return. Lucifer tests God, as always." Laoth stopped before a massive door halfway down a long hallway in the palace. The other two angels were still with us, silent. "We must fight until His return. Many more will fall." She tapped the door, and it opened.

A man stood there, dressed in pure white, with long hair pulled back and a face unlike any I'd ever seen. His eyes pulsed like lightning, his lips formed a straight expressionless line.

Fear swept over me. I fell to one knee.

"Stand up," the man demanded. "I'm no better than you, Elijah."

I staggered to my feet, brushing the dust off my black pants.

"It's good to see you both again." He glanced down at the baby. "And your child, Naomi. Have you given him the name?"

She shook her head, eyes wide. "Whenever the Lord shows me, I will."

"Do we know you?" I asked.

"This is Gabriel," Laoth said in reverence. Even she sounded awestruck. "He will take us to your brothers and sisters."

Gabriel's face was serene and flawless. "We are called

to a place where Lucifer would not expect us, because we go closer to him." He studied me. "You know this. I have shown you."

The dream. The expressionless face, the blazing eyes. My Mom had carried me past him, to the dragon, in Jerusalem. Doubt and fear washed over me. I remembered Don's haunting words: *He would make you a slave to his law. I will make you free.* I met the angel's gaze. "Do I have a choice?"

"Yes. Either you are faithful, or you are not." Gabriel paused. "The Lord will not force you."

I glanced at Naomi and her baby. Darkness awaited in Jerusalem. Maybe death.

She put her hand to my cheek. "What's wrong? We don't have to be afraid."

I smiled. She was right. No matter what awaited in Jerusalem, the greater risk was not obeying God, not being ready to stand before his throne. I turned to Gabriel again. "To Jerusalem?"

He nodded. "It is the magnet that tugs the hearts of your kind."

"What about the bomb?" The missile had been streaming toward the city. It should have hit just before the flare.

Gabriel motioned to Naomi.

"What happened?" I asked her.

"I followed along with your training for the war machines, remember?"

"Yeah, so?"

"I managed to hack into one, just to keep an eye out. We didn't know what Don was up to. When I saw the missile coming, I stopped it."

"Really?"

Her humble smile said yes. "It was a small thing. The other missiles would have hit, but I believe God stopped them all with the flare. He's giving people one more chance to repent."

"Pray it will be enough." Gabriel turned away. "We must go now."

We followed him out of the palace. I held up my hand, shielding my eyes from the bright morning sun. We were heading east.

"I thought we were going to Jerusalem?" It was the opposite direction.

He paused and stared at me. "We are, but this is the way. We go by foot to the Dead Sea first. You know why. Your dream showed you."

I remembered my Mom's words. I remembered my friend clutched in onyx claws. *Save Aisha from the dragon.* "We're going to find Aisha."

Gabriel nodded and continued toward the sun.

25

NAOMI AND I TREKKED with the four angels away from the palace and down a rocky path toward the Dead Sea. The land was a dry and empty desert. Hours passed without any sign of life outside our small group.

I found my gaze continually drifting back to the angels. Their bodies were human, but not. They wore light brown pants and hooded coats, with packs of supplies on their backs and gloves hiding their hands. But with each step their sleeves lifted, revealing a sliver of flesh and much more. Ribbons of light flowed out of their skin whenever I saw it, connecting in waves around them, and in wings behind them. Then the sleeve would fall, and it would be a large human in front of me again.

"You still can't see the wings?" I asked Naomi.

She shook her head. "They look like normal people to me. Strong, but normal."

"They are, that's what makes it so strange. Their wings aren't like feathers."

"Are they light, like you said Michael's are?"

"Exactly. It's the same as it is with the dragon, but bright instead of dark. The way they shimmer at their backs, lacing around their bodies—it's like part of them flows from another place."

"Maybe another dimension. They're spirit, not flesh." She paused and sipped from a canteen. "It sure would be nice to fly again, but I'm sure their reasons are good."

Gabriel stopped up ahead and turned to us. "Where exactly did the machine go down?"

"It should have crashed into the water about there." I pointed to a spot in the turquoise sea. "It was just barely past the shore, and already low, when I was ejected."

Gabriel led us to the shore, then turned north along an empty, dusty road. The angels' gazes swiveled from side to side, scouting the path ahead. Nothing else moved within sight.

"You really think Aisha could have survived the crash?" Naomi asked.

"The machine was built to withstand anything." I eyed the calm water, trying to summon hope. "I don't know what it would've been like inside, but Aisha saw the crash coming. She would've braced for it, put on a harness, or something."

"A harness? Why would the machine have one if it was

controlled by syncing?"

"She had to survive." I spoke with more confidence than I felt.

"Even if she lived through the landing, how would she get out after the machine sank?"

"I don't know, I guess—"

"Stay close," Gabriel called out in front of us.

Laoth and the other two angels pressed more tightly around Naomi and me, boxing us in. Far past Gabriel, where a river met the sea, I glimpsed a small group of people.

"Stay inside our circle," Gabriel said. "Many are lost and desperate. They might kill for food."

"The truck could be useful," one of the angels said. Laoth had introduced him as Cassiel. He was like an angel prototype—precise features, long blond hair, and bright blue eyes. All he lacked was a harp.

"What truck?" I strained to see.

The angel pointed to the group far ahead. Squinting, I realized there was a large shape beside the group. No way I would have known it was a truck from this distance.

"I bet they crashed it into the Jordan," Cassiel said. "It might have been working after the flare. Dumah and I can pull it out, maybe fix it." I glanced to the other angel, Dumah. He hadn't made a sound since he'd joined us. He looked nothing like the others—more like a nightclub bouncer, with a round face, flat nose, and thick neck.

"These people seem stranded," Laoth said. "We're a day's journey from Jerusalem, and the flare hit just hours ago. They must have been out here already."

"How many are there?" Naomi asked.

"Nine, that I can see now." Laoth put her hand on Gabriel's shoulder. "Maybe we can save them."

"Aisha could be with them," I added.

"I do not see her, but she could be in their vehicle." Gabriel's eyes stayed on the group. "God has put them in our path. And Cassiel is right. Anything without circuitry should be fixable. I believe it will be the old military truck, the one prepared for us."

"If you can fix the truck," Laoth said, "then Lucifer will be able to restore Babylon."

"Yes."

"How long do we have?" she asked.

Gabriel turned to her. "We can't know that."

"I know, but—"

"Nothing is going to survive long. We'll fight for Aisha and move on. We should be in Jerusalem by tomorrow."

"There are so many in trouble," Naomi said. "Why so much focus on Aisha?"

"The Lord has his reasons. Stay inside our circle." Gabriel marched ahead. I rushed to keep up with him, with Naomi close by my side. The baby slept.

"He's just focused on the mission," Laoth whispered beside us. "There's a reason God made him the messenger."

"I can hear you." Gabriel spoke without turning back.

Laoth smiled at us. "He's always listening . . . . You couldn't pray for a better angel to guide us."

Our group grew quiet after that, keeping up a steady pace along the road by the sea's edge. The angels seemed more tense with each mile. It made the hairs stand on the back of my neck.

After a while my legs began feeling the weight of the march. And I hadn't been the one carrying a baby. I leaned close to Naomi and asked, "Need a break?"

"No." She wiped her brow, leaving a streak through the dust.

"You sure?"

She nodded. "I'm a little tired, that's all."

I looked down at the infant's body. "Want me to hold him?"

She stopped walking and stared at me. The angels stopped, too. Even Gabriel. A long moment passed. The sun was falling over her left shoulder, nearing the horizon. "Maybe. It's worth a try." She looked to the angels. "He'll be hungry soon anyway. It might be a good idea to rest here a few minutes."

Gabriel had come to her side, and he was nodding. "We should still reach the group before sundown."

She began undoing the long cloth wound around her body. The baby burrowed his face into her chest.

I turned to face the sea as she nursed him. Nothing stirred the bright, serene surface. *Dead* Sea. It was hard to imagine so much water without any life in it. Even the sky seemed dead here, without birds around to dive in after fish.

"Elijah," Naomi said after a while. "Come here."

I went to her side and sat on the dusty ground. The boy was looking up at me. His big, curious eyes made me smile.

"Ready to hold him?" Naomi asked.

"Okay, I'll try."

"Be very gentle, very quiet. Make your arms into a cradle, like mine." I did it, feeling awkward as the angels watched with their half-stoic, half-amused faces. "Here, I will wrap him up."

I reached out my arms and Naomi gently handed him to me.

He began to whimper.

"What am I supposed to do?" I felt helpless as Naomi began coiling her cloth around the baby and me.

"Slide your arm through here," she instructed. The baby cried again. "Good," she said, "now through here." I put my arm through a gap in the fabric, and then Naomi tied something behind my back, synching the baby close to my chest. My arms were free, and he was staring up at me, wailing.

"Let's walk," Naomi said over his cries. "It might help."

"Waaa! Waaa!"

I rose to my feet.

He screamed at me. "Waaaaa!"

I took a step, then another.

"Waaa." Softer this time.

I hit my stride and the angels caught up and encircled us.

The boy whimpered, as if to show he still wasn't happy

about this, but he was willing to tolerate me. He yawned wide and fell quiet.

"He likes you!" Naomi said, looking down at him, then up at me. She was smiling, for the first time I'd seen in hours. There was a bounce to her step. It probably helped to shed the extra weight. My back already felt the difference.

"He's putting up with me," I said. "Are all babies so young this big?"

Naomi shrugged. "Not sure."

Laoth joined us. "This is better, with Elijah carrying him."

"I agree," Cassiel said. "If we're attacked, they can split up. That will divide any demons. Some might go for Naomi, while others go for the baby."

"Why would they go for me instead of him?" Naomi asked.

"Remember, there's no perfect unison between Lucifer and them," Laoth said. "They obey him out of fear, maybe adoration, but they can disobey, too. Some might not like that he's picked a daughter of man to be the mother of his child."

"Who else could he pick?" I asked.

"Another demon," said Cassiel.

"Or one of us." Laoth's voice was tense. "Not since the ancient days has spirit joined with flesh."

"The nephilim." Disgust filled Cassiel's perfect angel face. "They were the progeny of such unions. I hoped to never fight their kind again."

"You might be disappointed," Gabriel said. "I sense darkness ahead."

.

26

WE APPROACHED THE RIVER at a steady pace. The figures standing by its shore were not yet close enough for me to make out their faces. None of them seemed anything but human. Their stillness and raised guns told me what I needed to know. Apparently they couldn't see the angels for what they really were. I felt sure they'd be running if they saw four winged creatures approaching.

One of them shouted something at us. It sounded like Arabic. For the first time in a while, I missed my precept. Gabriel didn't slow, and we followed close.

The man shouted again and motioned a command. The group fanned out around him. I counted eleven of them—all black-robed men, no sign of Aisha. Just behind the men, a truck looked like it had crashed into the river. The back half of it was out of the water, covered in a desert-colored canopy. The men seemed to be guarding whatever was inside.

Gabriel continued ahead, despite the guns aimed at us. We were now within a stone's throw. The man in the center raised his gun and fired a shot into the sky. He shouted at us again. His long beard and dark eyes looked fierce. That was almost comforting, because it was human.

Gabriel turned his palms forward, lifted his arms, and said something. It must have been Arabic, too, because the group's apparent leader laughed. It was a laugh of disbelief, not humor.

The leader said something back, calmer this time, and all the others started laughing. The leader shook his head and glanced back at the truck. When he turned to us again, he leveled his gun at Gabriel and said a word. I felt sure it meant *stop*.

Gabriel stood still and straight as a fencepost, shaking his head as if sad. He pointed to the truck and said something, but it wasn't words. It was a deep groan, like stone grinding against stone, like the dragon's voice. The men cowered back, fear and confusion in their eyes. A few looked back at the truck, where Gabriel was pointing.

The back flap of canvas slid to the side, and a dark woman stepped out. Jezebel.

She showed no signs of harm from our attack on Patmos. Her black-scaled body sauntered up to the leader of the men. She leaned close to him, and her forked tongue slid out of her mouth as she whispered something in his ear. He craned his neck toward her.

I wanted to shout a warning, but I felt a sudden lump of jealousy in my chest that she would entice this man, and not me. The light of the setting sun made her body glow like molten lava. I stepped forward, but something held me in place. Laoth's grip was firm on my arm. It jarred me to my senses. *God help me.*

Gabriel moved ahead of us alone. He spoke in the same strange language, as if issuing a command. Then he drew a sword of blazing flame. He hadn't been carrying a sword. It seemed pulled from another place, like his wings.

Jezebel, still pressed close to the man, put her hand on the curve of her hip. "A pleasure as always, Gabriel," she said, pronouncing his name like it was forbidden fruit. "The Master looks forward to seeing you. He says it's been too long. Give me the child and the seer, and you may leave without pain."

Gabriel replied in the strange language, with more words than before. Whatever he said made Jezebel take a step back, though her pose remained confident.

"You'll have to kill all of them," she said. "You've had your time on earth. This is *our* time." She ducked behind the leader of the group, and they unleashed fire at us.

In a blink, Gabriel, Laoth, and Cassiel flashed ahead. Dumah wrapped Naomi and me tight in his arms, so that his broad body covered ours completely. I couldn't see past him, but I heard the gunshots. I heard the bullets hitting Dumah's back like dull thuds, his grunts of pain, and the screams beyond him.

The gunshots stopped. A heavy rumbling replaced them, like an avalanche crashing toward us. Dumah stood and turned. His back bore a hundred dark holes. Blood soaked through his shirt. The giant angel staggered as he stepped forward.

Up ahead, an army of dark little creatures surrounded the angels. Gabriel and Laoth moved among them like flickering flames in a bed of coals. But the coals were moving, too, roiling chaos up to the angels' waists. Cassiel was facedown on the ground. None of the men were still standing. Jezebel stood on the back of the truck, with her arms held out parallel to the ground, like a sorceress commanding her minions.

Gabriel swung his flaming blade in a low arc, splitting a dozen of the dark creatures in half. As they fell, more flooded into the space.

And more were coming at us.

Naomi and I backed away as Dumah charged forward. He hit the creatures like a boulder against ants. They flew back, but came again. Their black, spindly arms grabbed at his legs. One of them leapt onto his back. It looked like a short, burnt tree come to life, and it stabbed its arms down into Dumah's flesh.

He did not slow. Neither did the fiends.

Dumah reached Laoth, and the two of them pressed together into the swarm. They carved a path to the truck. Jezebel leapt away, into the river. Dumah dove after her, and Laoth turned back to us.

Naomi and I had nowhere to run. The creatures swept

toward us. Their eyes were pale and red and feverish. They had no mouths, no noses. They looked frail, as if their limbs were twigs that would snap.

"What's happening?" Naomi asked, terrified.

She couldn't see them. "Evil, dark things. They're fighting the angels . . . and charging at us." Running wouldn't work. They were too fast. "Here." I held out the baby to Naomi. He was eerily silent, eyes wide open. "Stay down and pray. I'll fight."

She nodded and curled into a ball on the ground. None of the creatures were going to reach her and the child without going through me first.

God, give me strength. Protect us.

One of the creatures dashed forward. It came up only to my waist, but its body struck like a whip around my legs. I fell, and immediately they were on me. Thrashing and stabbing, like barbed wire yanked over my skin.

I tried to jerk my arms away, but the creatures pinned me down. I watched in terror as they swarmed over Naomi's back.

This wasn't how it was supposed to end. *God, save her! Please—*

Laoth landed beside me. The darkness cringed back. She whirled in a blur of light, blazing through the fiends like a flame through kindling. Moments later they were gone. She was helping me to my feet.

Just beyond us, at the rear of the truck, Gabriel was kneeling over Cassiel's motionless body.

27

A CRY SLIPPED from Laoth's mouth, and she rushed to Cassiel's side. She held her hand to his face. Naomi and I approached the three of them. Each step made my back burn in pain.

"Can you save him?" Naomi asked.

Laoth looked up at us, with tears in her eyes. "He's asleep now."

"Asleep?"

"Not for long," Gabriel said, sliding his arms under Cassiel's lifeless body. He lifted him easily and faced the river. "I will take him away."

"I saw Dumah taking bullets, but he survived." I swallowed. "So what happened to Cassiel?"

"Jezebel . . ." Laoth kept her eyes on Gabriel, carrying

the angel away. "She got Cassiel before we could stop her. The others were like twisted nephilim. The worst kind."

"What did they look like?" Naomi sounded confused. "I thought the nephilim were giants."

"Some were," Laoth said, "when angels were the fathers. These are spawn of hell. Forced breeds." She paused. "I will say no more of them."

Naomi looked to me. "I saw only dark blurs around us, almost like vapor. What did you see?"

"There were so many of them. Hundreds, but each one so small, like an army of little goblins, except their faces had no mouths or noses, only eyes. Evil eyes. Their bodies were spindly and sharp as thorns."

"Lucifer has many creatures in his domain," Laoth said, turning to us. The hardness of her eyes told us the discussion was over. "Speaking of it only worsens the devil's tools. Fear. Horror. We should pray now for healing, for light."

She turned to face Dumah, who was walking toward us with a woman cradled in his arms. The woman's body looked like a raven's feather against his bright skin. Four other women and a little girl were trailing behind. I could see only their eyes through the black cloth covering them from head to foot, but that was enough to see shock and despair.

Gabriel showed up again at Laoth's side. "It's getting dark, and the group needs rest before we journey to Jerusalem. The trip is short, but not without obstacles. Tend to everyone now. We'll camp here, by the river. I'll make sure the area's safe and prepare some food." Laoth nodded, and Gabriel glided off, his head turning from one end of the horizon to the other, then up to the cloudless sky.

"Elijah," Laoth said, putting her hands to my back. "You're hurt."

I nodded.

She tilted her head up. *"Jehovah Rapha . . . ."* She continued in words I didn't understand. Her lips moved delicately, but intensely. Her hands moved over my back, and I could *feel* the light from her washing over me. Something poured into me like a rush of cold water.

My back clenched, then released. I stretched my arms out. No pain. I turned to Laoth in awe. "What did you do?"

"Nothing," she said. "But the Lord answered my prayer."

Dumah and the group of women were watching us. "Elijah?" asked a woman's faint, familiar voice. She was in Dumah's thick arms. "Is that you?"

Our eyes met. Dark, almond eyes.

"Aisha!" I rushed to her. "You survived!"

Her face was pale, her body motionless. "Barely," she said. "I got hurt badly in the crash. I haven't felt my legs since, but I managed to paddle my way to the shore."

"That's amazing," Naomi said. "How many lives do you have left?"

"This might be my last one." Aisha nodded to the women behind Dumah. "They found me by the water."

"Wh-why?" one of the women asked, her voice breaking, her accent thick. "Aisha, who is this people?"

"They are friends," Aisha answered. "They will protect us. We are safe now."

The woman placed her face in her hands, sobbing. The other women and the little girl gathered around her, crying with her.

Aisha reached out and touched my arm. "Shanti is the only one who speaks a little English. The leader of the men who died was her husband. The others are all family. Brothers, cousins. These women are the grandmother, two sisters, and a daughter."

"What are they doing out here?" I asked.

"They were fleeing from Jerusalem. It's bad there. Very bad. They were close by when our headquarters detected my tracker heading straight for the Dead Sea. Headquarters sent the men to look for me."

"What headquarters? You don't mean in Tehran—" I caught myself. The city was gone. Probably most people Aisha knew were dead.

She was shaking her head. "The Mahdi's backup base in Jerusalem. All this happened before that flash wiped out the network. I'd probably be dead if these men and women hadn't come to me. The men were not saints, but they didn't deserve whatever just happened. I think some of them sensed that the woman they picked up was trouble, but the leader insisted on bringing her. Who was she?"

"Jezebel," I said. "A demon."

Aisha's eyes opened wide, but she nodded as if she

believed it. "The demon must have known what was coming and tricked the men into taking them with her. She looked like a nice, quiet woman . . ." Aisha breathed out heavily. "Why is this happening? What else have you seen?"

Where to start? Everything from Don's palace seemed like a distant nightmare now. "I saw a huge flash," I said. "Just before the Mahdi's nukes hit, we think there was a solar flare. It knocked out all electricity, the satellite systems, everything."

"Makes sense, I guess. My precept has been totally gone since the crash. It had to have been something massive to wipe it out. The Mahdi's attack might have stopped *Dajjal* if not for this."

"That's ridiculous," Naomi glared at Aisha. "You're still thinking like that? The Mahdi's attack would have killed millions of innocent people."

Aisha's body may have been broken, but her eyes blazed with life. "My brother died trying to save people like you."

"I'm sorry for your loss," Naomi said, hardly sounding sorry. "These are the end times. I told you weapons would be no use."

"We each fight evil in our own way."

"You can't fight evil with evil. And what was the cost?"

Aisha didn't answer, but she grimaced as she glanced to her legs. Naomi was right—millions of lives lost, cities blown away, bodies shattered, and for what? Don had survived. Awkward silence mounted as the two of them stared at each other, my love and my friend. I wondered if this had been their dispute all along. Was that why Aisha had warned me about Naomi in the beginning?

Laoth had left and returned. Now she glided between us. "Aisha, I am Laoth." Her voice was gentle as a forest stream. "Elijah told us we might find you here. He wouldn't let us leave you."

"Thank you." Aisha smiled at me.

"We'll take care of you," Laoth continued, "and your new friends. Untainted souls must find what peace we can."

Aisha nodded. Naomi did, too.

Laoth pointed to the truck by the riverbank. "Dumah, take these women there. We'll set camp." She turned to me. "Elijah, can you gather wood for a fire?"

I said I would, and we parted soon after that. I found a few low bushes scattered around the river. Not much wood, but it would have to be enough. The demons could come again. Night was falling.

28

OUR BATTERED GROUP clustered around a small fire. I sat slumped between Naomi and Aisha, my body exhausted. Dumah was off to the side, peering under the hood of the truck, trying to fix its engine. Gabriel was close to the fire, leaning over a spit of roasting fish. Laoth was holding the little Arabic girl, who stared up at her in wonder.

A question had been eating at me. "Aisha, did you hear Gabriel speaking when we first reached your group?"

"I think so. Why?"

"It sounded like Arabic, and it made the men laugh. But Gabriel doesn't seem like the joking type."

"It wasn't a joke," Naomi said. "I'm pretty sure he offered to help the men pull the truck from the river."

"Maybe, but why do you think that?"

"Because I was praying for it." She looked past me, to Aisha. "Am I right?"

Aisha nodded. "He told the group's leader that he could save them. Then he said he could lift the truck for them."

"Lift it?" I laughed. "They shouldn't have doubted him."

Aisha's eyes tracked Gabriel as he served fish to the other women. "That's what he did, too, with the other angel's help, the quiet one. While you were gathering wood and Naomi was nursing her baby, the two of them walked straight up to the truck, grabbed it by the back hitch, and dragged it out of the river like it was a plastic toy."

"We are safe with them," Naomi said.

Aisha shook her head. "It doesn't make sense. I mean, I believe Elijah, but what are angels doing here, with us? Why aren't they attacking Dajjal?"

"They—" Naomi began, but stopped short as Gabriel approached.

He was carrying a small stack of roasted fish laid over a cloth. He knelt before Aisha and gently handed her a piece of fish. Then he gave one to Naomi, and one to me. "Try it," he encouraged.

Naomi, Aisha, and I shared a glance. Did they think this was as strange as I did—being served dinner by the messenger of God? I reminded myself they couldn't see the light arcing from his back like an elaborate halo.

"You must be hungry," Gabriel said. "Please, eat."

I looked down at the fish. It smelled delicious. I pinched off a small bite with my fingers. The savory piece melted in my mouth.

"So?" Gabriel asked, rising to his feet.

"It's wonderful," Naomi said. "Where did you get it?"

"The Jordan." Gabriel pointed to the dark ribbon of water behind us. "It will be the last fish you eat here."

"Why's that?" Aisha asked.

"Revelation speaks of the death of every living thing in the sea." The angel winced as if the words brought pain. "Those warnings have come to pass. Zephaniah spoke the truth, too:

'I will utterly sweep away everything
from the face of the earth,' declares the Lord.
'I will sweep away man and beast;
I will sweep away the birds of the heavens
and the fish of the sea,
and the rubble with the wicked.
I will cut off mankind
from the face of the earth,' declares the Lord.

"This is what comes next?" Naomi's face had gone pale.

"Yes," Gabriel answered.

"Will you sit with us?" Aisha asked.

Gabriel looked over his shoulder. Laoth was still holding the little girl and speaking with the other women.

"Okay," Gabriel said, turning back. He sat down with us like any person would, crossing his legs and unfurling a cloth around the last fish. He took a bite. "You're right, not bad, though I prefer the fish in Galilee." He pinched off another piece.

"I heard you dragged the truck out of the river," I said.

"Dumah and I did it." Gabriel looked to Aisha. "Our strength has limits, but we are fighting evil with all the powers we have. Just as good comes in many forms, so does evil. It cannot be fought with only swords and bombs."

Aisha nodded, her eyes open in wonder.

"Can one of you heal Aisha's legs?" Naomi asked.

Gabriel shook his head slowly. "We cannot, but God can. Pray that he does and he will in his time." He glanced at Dumah. "The truck will be working by the morning, so all of you can ride."

"Where will we go?" Aisha asked.

"There's only one real option." The angel turned to me. I felt bare under his gaze, like he was looking at me from the inside out.

"We can't go east," Aisha said. "It's desert for miles, and beyond that will be only contaminated land. My people's land."

"What if we followed the river north?" Naomi asked. "It's the Jordan, after all. We'll have water, and the order used to have a small base by the Sea of Galilee."

"Elijah?" Gabriel's eyes had never left me. "Tell them what you've seen."

"You mean a dream? I've had many lately."

"You know which one I mean." Gabriel sounded patient and calm, but I felt like he was channeling my mind toward an answer. Kind of like Azazel, but much gentler. Naomi and Aisha watched me, waiting.

"It was a couple weeks ago," I began. "I was an infant, carried into a smoldering city. Towers were all around me. They were like spokes up into the sky with little eggs stacked on their sides. But the eggs were empty. The streets were empty. I went to the Dome of the Rock." I glanced at the angel, and he nodded. "I passed Gabriel on the way. He was wearing the most dazzling white. But the darkness over the Dome was greater. The dragon was perched there."

I looked to Aisha, then to Naomi. They weren't going to like this, but with Gabriel beside me, I felt like I had no choice but to continue. I closed my eyes, seeing it again.

"The dragon watched me approach. It held my uncle Jacob in one of its claws, and Aisha in the other."

"*Me?*" Aisha asked.

I kept my eyes closed. I continued.

"I was crying. The dragon bowed its neck down, revealing Don Cristo. He grabbed me and dangled me in front of the dragon's eyes. The dragon stretched out its jaws and swallowed me whole. I slid down its throat and into its belly. Inside was another child. It was Naomi's son, glowing with dazzling light. Then everything exploded."

"You never told me that last part." Naomi's voice trembled. "What do you mean it exploded?"

I opened my eyes. "I don't know. It just exploded. Everything ended after that."

"You think this will happen?" Naomi asked, staring at Gabriel.

"I do not know all God's reasons. But I deliver all his messages." The angel's eyes settled on me. "Your dreams frighten you. They test you, and you have not run from them yet. You find your way into them."

As clear as an angel could be. It had to mean we were on track to reach Jerusalem, to face the dragon. "When we go to the city, will you come with us?"

"Yes. You have prayed for our protection. You will have it. Friends of yours are waiting there."

Friends. For some reason the word made me think of school, of Adam and Hoff and the others. I hadn't seen them since the sailboat. They would have gone to Babylon. Now where would they be?

Aisha's voice interrupted my thoughts. "Your dream. It was Jerusalem?"

I looked from her to Naomi. "Yes."

Naomi tilted her head down at her sleeping child, clutched tight to her chest. "To Jerusalem," she whispered. "It all ends in Jerusalem. God, please give us strength."

29

WE BROKE CAMP at sunrise. The light streamed over
the low cliff on the opposite side of the river, making even
the dry brown land around us seem golden. Gabriel was
standing at the river's edge, his face toward the sun. Laoth
held Aisha and was helping the other women into the back
of the truck. Dumah started the engine.

"It's time!" Laoth called out.

Gabriel turned and began walking to her. His face was
radiant, glorious. As he passed, he glanced at me
knowingly, no doubt seeing the wonder in my eyes. "Let
the Lord shine His face upon you, too. Come on, you'll
ride in the front with Dumah and Naomi."

"What about you?" I asked, following after him to the
truck.

"I'll be on top."

Right, so he'd just cling to the roof.

He ignored my skeptical look. "Comfort Naomi," he said softly. "She is afraid, though she won't admit it. Even with her strong faith, she can have doubts. And speak up if you see anything dark. Do you understand?"

"Got it."

"Good." He opened the passenger door. "Hop in. I'll bring Naomi."

I climbed inside. Dumah was sitting behind the wheel, huge and silent as always.

"Good morning."

He nodded. No words.

"So, how'd you get the truck to work?"

He didn't blink, didn't flinch. He reached over to me, put his powerful hand on my shoulder, and gave it a light squeeze. Was that a tiny curl of his lip? Maybe he thought it was funny. But then he put his hands back on the wheel and looked out the windshield. So much for talking to Dumah.

Naomi joined us soon after that, holding the baby. "Good morning."

"You look beautiful."

She laughed. "Must have been that sweet beauty sleep. I found a great spot between a few rocks."

I slid over to the middle of the seat. "Where have you been?" I asked as she climbed in. Her makeshift bed had been empty when Laoth woke me.

"Praying." She pointed outside the truck, up a hill to

the right. "There's a magnificent view. You can see where the Jordan meets the Dead Sea, and the desert stretches as far as you can see to the east. The sun rose over the barren hills and dunes into the distance, making them yellow and amber and pink. We've taken our sunrises for granted."

"You think this will all be gone soon?"

She shook her head. "No, it's all going to be replaced. It's going to be far better. I want to remember the beauty here, so I can fully appreciate the difference."

"You mean the new heavens and the new earth? I read something about that."

She nodded. "Think of what we've seen. Angels of the Lord, here with us. I have faith in His Word. He will come again, and soon."

"Like today soon?"

A tap on the top of the truck interrupted us. Gabriel's head appeared, upside down, in front of us. He motioned to Dumah and pulled his head away. Dumah slammed his foot on the gas. We surged forward over the rough terrain. I pressed back against the seat and put on my seatbelt. Naomi did the same, then hugged the baby at her chest.

With Dumah's hands on the wheel and foot on the pedal, we dodged a thousand boulders and cracks in the hard ground. It wasn't long before we reached a road. We wheeled left onto it, heading west. A sign said something in Arabic, but at least it had a number I could read: "1." The road into Jerusalem.

The jarring bumps ceased. The truck's tires churned smooth pavement. "Why so fast?" I asked, finally able to speak without my jaw shaking.

Dumah of course gave no answer. "I think Gabriel told him to hurry," Naomi said. "Another angel visited him early this morning. There must have been a message."

"Another angel? How do you know?"

"I saw him beside Gabriel, and then an instant later he was gone, like a flash of light."

I remembered something like it on Patmos months ago. "What if it was Jesus?"

"It could have been," she said, excited. "You asked if I thought today might be the last day, and I've been thinking about it. This really could be it. Why not?"

"The earth has had a lot of days. Today is, what, something in late December? What's so special about that?"

"Think about Don," she said. "You're always telling me he's trying to take what God created and twist it. Wouldn't he want to make Jerusalem his last stand?"

"There are a lot of prophecies and theories about the city."

"No, it's not that. God cares about everything, not just one city, not even Jerusalem. The order thinks the end could happen anywhere, and actually, that it will happen everywhere."

"So why would Don set himself up in Jerusalem? Why would my dream have been there?"

"All who believe in God revere the city. We have the cross—it's the city where Jesus died and rose again. The Jewish people have the Western Wall. The Muslims have the Dome of the Rock, where they think Muhammad rose to heaven. What better place for Don to try to declare, once and for all, that he is god of the earth?"

"Maybe," I said. There was a logic to it. "But you think Jesus will come again here just because Don is here?"

"I think the Lord will come everywhere, all at once."

The truck swerved hard right, swiping past a burnt-out car on the side of the road. I saw figures far ahead. People walking along the road. It made me think of the dream with my Mom, of the bodies piled up below the towers in Jerusalem.

"What about the baby?" I asked. "What do you think my dream means?"

Naomi didn't answer at first. She looked down at her son, and he looked up at her. "We all have our role. I never expected to have this precious boy. I still think his innocence holds some answer to Don's plans. Don doesn't know God's plan, but we don't exactly know it, either. I'm praying that God will show me my role, and that I will have the strength to do it."

The truck began to slow.

I looked ahead as more people came into view. The brownish-white hills steepened around us, and the dark figures became all the more clear. I saw the people wore scraps for clothing, or nothing at all. Their heads were shaved bald, like Alexi's. Most of them had nothing on their backs. Not a weapon was in sight.

One man carried a little girl on his shoulders. The bottoms of her feet were black and bloody. I imagined those little feet submerged in fluid, trapped in a capsule, while the girl's mind flipped about in childish fantasies for weeks—chocolate and candy, princesses and ponies—until her impulses drove her deeper and deeper in her quest for satisfaction. However far her mind had descended, yesterday her dreamworld bubble must have popped. The capsule would have opened, and the little girl would have somehow climbed down a tower until her pale and pruned feet touched the ground. Those little feet were no match for this black pavement.

Blank stares met us as we passed. Men and women continued in the opposite direction and looked as if they wanted nothing to do with the city we approached.

Eventually I closed my eyes, unable to bear what I saw. "It makes no sense. They're not even trying to stop us."

"They're broken . . . defeated," Naomi replied.

My eyes opened. I winced at a sight on the left side of the road. Two bodies, a child's beside a woman's, facedown on the pavement, with black birds flocking around them. I tried to keep my mouth shut, hoping Naomi wouldn't notice. She was gazing out the other side of the truck.

"This is the apocalypse," she whispered. "It's not chaos, not fighting. It's despair, souls robbed of their will to live. Don did it. He hauled them into his virtual world, he harvested their bodies." Tears had filled her eyes. "Just look at them."

We passed a family on the right. The father held a motionless child. The mother clung to him, on her knees, while four naked children huddled behind her.

"We have to do something." Naomi turned to me, wet streaks down her face. Her eyes passed to Dumah. "Please, can't we stop and help?"

The angel's fists were tight on the wheel, but he turned his head just a fraction toward us. Tears streamed from his eyes, too. He shook his head once, then looked ahead again.

"Please Lord," Naomi prayed, "come soon."

30

WE PASSED HUNDREDS, thousands, as we made our way up the hill that ringed Jerusalem's eastern border. We couldn't see the city on the other side of the hill, but we could see Don's towers. Dozens of them stabbed hundreds of feet into the sky. The towers of Babylon.

We were halfway up the hill when Dumah turned off the highway.

"Where are we going?" Naomi asked.

Dumah didn't answer.

"This is the West Bank." I eyed the decaying apartment buildings around us. Their white plaster wore the dirt of decades. "The people here have suffered for years. I remember coming here once with my Mom and Dad, when I was little. We brought toys and candy for the kids. They were poor but happy. It's weird, but I remember thinking they seemed happier than I was. Does that make sense?"

"Kids don't care about things like money," Naomi said. "I think that's one of the reasons Jesus told us to be like them. They can be happy without a thing in the world. They just want to explore and find adventure and be loved."

"I bet you were a happy kid."

"Happy as I could be." She stared down at her sleeping baby. "My dad walked away from the money and the fame. He cared more about us than all that."

"My dad had it backwards."

"Most people do." The truck rounded a switchback curve.

"But he still did good things," I said. "I think he always felt a little guilty about his fortune. It was different with my mom. She cared about the people, and her loyalty to this land ran deep. She was the one who suggested coming here with the toys. The kids were so happy, running everywhere, throwing the balls we gave them. Now look at these buildings. It feels like a ghost town."

The truck climbed a steep road and entered a tight cluster of apartments. One of Don's spires loomed ahead, on the crest of the hill. Naomi spoke softly: "I guess they all went to Babylon. Remember the video we saw in Don's palace? His machines moved their bodies into these towers. How do you think they got down?"

"They climbed. Some might have jumped."

"But not all," Gabriel said, appearing beside Naomi's

open window. "People have a little longer to repent." He pointed to a building ahead. "We are pulling into this garage. Laoth, Dumah, and I will join our kind, securing the perimeter. Go to the fourth floor. You will stay here tonight."

"What's going on?" Naomi asked.

"Your father will tell you more." With that, the angel's face disappeared from view and the truck rolled to a stop. Dumah hopped out of the truck and we did the same.

Naomi and I went to the back of the truck to get the women. I pulled back the canvas flap.

Aisha's tired eyes met mine. "Where are we?"

"We're not sure, but it sounds like this building is a safe place." I paused, glancing down at Aisha's legs as the other Muslim women climbed out, talking quietly in Arabic.

She nodded to me, and we understood each other. I picked her up. She was light, her small frame hanging fragile in my arms. The group of us entered the building, walked up four flights of stairs, and found ourselves on a plain balcony.

I took a few steps forward, realizing there were at least a dozen doors. I looked back to Naomi. "Gabriel didn't say which door we should enter."

She was studying the first door. Number 41. "It must not matter," she said. "Let's try this one." She knocked.

Moments later the door cracked open. Naomi gave a little shout and dashed through. The women filed in after her. I carried Aisha in last.

Naomi was in her father Moses's arms. I couldn't tell if

she was laughing or crying. Maybe both, but she sounded happy. His huge hands held tight to her and the baby.

Beyond them, the room was open for the entire floor of the apartment building. A hundred cots were lined up in rows along the walls. In the center was a makeshift circle of folding chairs.

"Elijah!"

I turned toward the familiar voice. Brie swept me into her arms, squeezing Aisha between us. Her long blonde hair smelled of fresh soap, making me realize how filthy we were.

"You made it out!" She released me and smiled down at Aisha. "Sorry about that. I'm Brie. What's your name?"

"Aisha."

"I've heard a lot about you," Brie said. "Come, please, we were just about to eat. Are you hungry?"

Brie and others sprang into a flurry of motion. One woman spoke Arabic to the group with us. Whatever she said made them smile. A man gently took Aisha in his arms and carried her to the other side of the room, where others were getting medical help.

Brie escorted Naomi and me into the center of the room. We joined several others who were sitting there. I breathed easier knowing we'd found another hideout of the order, but despite the warm welcome, I couldn't shake the feeling that we'd entered a war shelter.

"How many leaders are left?" I asked. Don had wanted them all dead.

Moses sighed. "Two."

"My husband Chris is in Jerusalem, over the hill," Brie said. "He's trying to build alliances with the remaining faithful, or with anyone who will oppose Don. Many Jewish and Muslim people have joined us. Few doubt that the end is coming soon."

"Which other leader is still alive?"

Brie and Moses exchanged a look. They didn't answer.

"We saw Ronaldo in Don's palace." Naomi's voice held a hint of dread.

Moses put his hand on her shoulder. "We lost him."

My throat tightened. I tried to swallow but couldn't. "How?"

Brie spoke: "When Don staged his last attack on Tehran, a few of us made it into his palace with drones. We made it to the wing where Ronaldo and others were imprisoned. We managed to blow open a couple doors, and inside one of them, we . . . found Ronaldo." She swallowed. "He had already joined the Lord."

Naomi sniffed and wiped her eyes. Moses held her tight. I tried not to think about that brutal guard being sent into the prison cell of a man in shackles. I wouldn't think about the cheery Brazilian on a sailboat, or about his ukulele and bare feet and open smile. I wouldn't think about where I'd be without him, or about the tears filling my eyes. No, I wouldn't think any of those things. Not now.

"I'm so sorry," Brie continued. "There was nothing we could do after that. It was just moments before Don's machines were on us. They blew through our drones like wildfire."

"The doors," I said slowly. "When you blew them open—what else did you find?"

"Not much," Brie answered. "Another prisoner was there. He was in good, strong shape, but I didn't even catch his name before my drone was taken out. I doubt he made it."

I saw in my mind those fiery eyes behind prison doors. "You may have helped save us."

"How?"

"Don had locked up angels there. It wasn't a normal prison. He had demons on guard. Ronaldo told us they could have been detained like the Prince of Persia had once detained Michael."

"I prayed God would work through our defeat," Moses said, looking to Brie. "We knew He could use our loss for gain. I bet that man you released was an angel. Maybe he released the others."

"It's possible," Brie mused.

"After the flare, the angels brought us to you," Naomi said. "They looked like normal people to me, but Elijah could see hints of their spirit form."

The group of them looked to me. I nodded, glancing around at the new faces. The others had been listening to us quietly. "You said another leader is alive?"

"I am." It was an old Asian man. His beard hung to his knees like a spindly waterfall. "My name is Zhang Tao." He was studying me knowingly.

Something about his gaze made me relax. "Have we

met?"

"Briefly," Naomi said. "In the order's hideaway, the one in the cave, Zhang Tao was there."

"He is our wisest leader," Moses added.

"The oldest, at least." Zhang Tao grinned. "I will tell you my story."

31

"OUR CHURCH WAS among the order's strongest," Zhang Tao began. "In China, the government was always against us, much as it was in your country, but with a firm rod to enforce the law. We had no option but to rely on each other and to trust in God. For every person the government killed, two converts took the martyr's place. We praised God for it, as Peter told us to do. *Rejoice when grieved by trials, so that the tested genuineness of your faith—more precious than gold that perishes though it is tested by fire—may be found to result in praise and glory and honor at the revelation of Jesus Christ.*

"Our church grew to millions, and grew more. We reached one hundred million, and then even the government had to let us be. Oh, they forced us to be quiet in the ways of today—we had no precepts, no connections to the global mind—but we grew through something purer. We showed our neighbors what we were. The countryside of China became our domain, for few who saw the love of Christ in us could resist the Lord's call."

"How did you end up here?" I asked.

The old man's wrinkled face went somber. "This is a sad tale." He looked to Moses. The two of them seemed to communicate without a word. Eventually Moses nodded, and Zhang Tao spoke on. "We do not run from sad tales, for we know the world is fallen. We learn from the suffering, we grow from the trials."

He gazed at the floor, his eyes distant as he ran his bony hand along his beard. "It begins with the love of my life. Her name was Xi. Her beauty rivaled the sun. Her energy—" he smiled toward Naomi— "it was like yours. We married fifty-nine years ago, in 2007. We had five children. We raised them in Guangzhou, in our home by the beautiful lake. Our children grew as our church did— slowly at first, and then all at once into adulthood."

He paused, staring at me. "I have known the joy of a rich, full life. That is why I know now the meaning of pain and suffering. Remember, Elijah, what does our enemy want most?"

"To take God's place?"

"Yes, and that means in everyone's soul, too. Think of how he does that. First he must make us weak. He hates God for creating us. He hates us for being free in a way he cannot be. Through many years he has mastered the art of stealing our freedom. For some, he uses pleasure and abundance. For me, he destroyed half of my soul. The devil stole Xi from me. It drove me to anger. I have confessed, even forgiven, but still I feel the anger surge up within me, like a fire I can barely contain." He closed his eyes and fell silent, but his hands clenched into fists, shaking.

"What happened?"

His eyes opened and met mine with a fierce edge. "You see to the heart of things, Elijah. The devil would not be content to let us die in peace, or even in pain. He attacked on a perfect Sunday morning. The spring cherry blossoms dusted the shores of the lake by my church. As I taught our people, Xi sat in the front, smiling at me, encouraging me as always. Don stormed in with a force from the Chinese military. They slaughtered everyone who would not bow to him. Two thousand three hundred sixty-four died. But not Xi. Don made me watch as he extracted memories from her precept. He stole everything she'd seen and heard and lived—our wedding night, every anniversary, every secret. Then Don transferred the memories to a young woman who was with him and, with his eyes on me, he slit Xi's throat. Androids held me, made me watch, as her life spilled out."

Tears filled the old man's eyes. He started to say more, but his voice broke.

Brie put her arm around his shoulder. "You don't have to talk about this."

"I do. Elijah must know." His sad gaze turned back to me. "You will be the one with a chance to speak, and your soul must understand suffering to tell it right. The souls of millions, maybe billions, could be saved." He pressed his eyes closed, sighed deeply, then continued. "That day, the young woman who stood beside Don wore a slim, silk red dress. She looked at me as Xi had. I knew her, and she knew me. 'Zhang Tao,' she said, with all the affection I'd known of my wife. 'You were always weak. You will never have the strength of my love,' she taunted, and then she turned to Don Cristo and kissed him. He called her Xing Xing."

Xing Xing. The woman who'd been in Don's tower in Geneva. The rich Chinese woman who had known Don. "Do you know what happened to her after that?" I asked.

"The woman was the daughter of China's leading general. I think Don used her to cement his influence with my country's government. The woman had all the life-force of my Xi, and all her memories, but with a soul hollowed out for evil. Don became her only desire, her only end." Zhang Tao paused, breathed deep. "Never has my faith been so tested. I think Don did not kill me that day only because he hoped this torture would break me and turn me from God. That would be a greater victory to him than my martyrdom with the rest. But Don underestimates the Lord. He always has. God gave me strength. He used this trial to refine me. Never have my prayers been so focused, so intent on defeating the evil one."

The group fell silent after that. Eventually Naomi spoke. "What will you do next?"

"I will join the order's last warriors in battle," Zhang

Tao said. "It is a battle we will lose, but we fight because we must. As long as such evil reigns, we live to defeat it. Our Christ is a warrior king."

"But . . ." I tried to find the right words. How could I ask this man, whose ancient body had no strength left in it, how he could expect to challenge Don. "How will you fight?"

He rose to his feet, swaying slightly. He bent forward and lowered to his knees. He closed his eyes, clasped his hands together, and raised his head to the ceiling. "Like this."

"Prayer?" I couldn't shake my skepticism. "Hasn't the order been praying against Don all along?"

Zhang Tao nodded. "And we won't ever stop."

"The order will pray to give you cover," Moses said.

"Cover for what? I'm not leaving you again." Naomi frowned at him the way only a daughter can at her dad. "Where would we go anyway?"

Zhang Tao was staring at me. Moses and Brie turned to me as well.

"Well?" Naomi asked again.

My words came out more confident than I felt. "We go to face Don and the dragon in Jerusalem."

Naomi gripped her son tighter. "I know about your dream," she said, "but how do we know if it means we're supposed to go that far? We're safer here. Why walk into Don's hands?"

"Naomi, our goal is not simply survival," Zhang Tao answered. "We must seek to glorify God. The Lord seems to have shown Elijah where you are called to go. Perhaps you have a special role to play in the end. You will rest here a while, then you'll leave with an escort of unseen angels and prayers." He rose from his knees. "From the four corners of the earth, the order will pray for you. I pray with the righteous fury of a man tortured by Satan and saved by Christ. I pray until my last breath, when I will drift like a blossom in the wind to my Xi's side, where she rests with our Savior." He let out a sigh, his face softening. "But before that, let's share a meal and sleep. Let's enjoy these little blessings that remain on earth."

32

"ONE MORE DAY, one more night, and then your time will come, Elijah."

Gabriel stood before me, relaxed and joyous. His face shone brighter than I remembered. "Run the race with endurance," he said. "When you reach this place, you will want to say, as Paul did: *I have fought the good fight, I have finished the race, I have kept the faith.*"

Behind the angel was a round gate of pure white. It stood in the middle of a wall that loomed high above and stretched from one horizon to the other. The foot of the wall had the red luster of the earth, above that was a stretch of blue sapphire, and all the way up were stripes of more jeweled color.

"Where are we?" I asked.

"We are in the place that is to come."

I remembered what I'd read months ago, at sail with Ronaldo. The pearl gate, the immense wall of precious stones. "The new heaven and the new earth?"

Gabriel nodded. "He sent me to show you this, to give you hope." The angel clasped my shoulder and looked deep into my eyes. "The last mile of the race is the hardest."

"But you're protecting us."

His expression became solemn. "I cannot save you, any of you. None of us wish for pain, but sin will not perish without a fight."

"Sin? You mean Don Cristo?"

"Both."

I began drifting back, away from Gabriel and the gate and the wall. "Wait," I said. "Can't you tell me more?"

"Keep the faith. Finish the race." The angel lifted his arm in farewell.

The ground rushed beneath my feet. A gale wind blew behind me, whipping my hair forward. I glanced back to a cyclone of clouds and lightning. It was sucking me in.

I tried to step forward, but the pull of the storm was too great. It erupted around me. The beautiful wall and gate were gone. The storm swallowed me whole and spit me out on a cot in an apartment building outside Jerusalem.

I sat up. The room was dark, quiet.

The cot beside mine was empty. Naomi was gone. I felt a rush of panic but breathed deeply. She had to be safe.

This was the order's place. A prayed-in place. I rose and walked out one of the doors to the building's balcony.

Two figures were to my right. As I approached them, I breathed easier. It was Moses and Naomi.

"Want to watch the dawn with us?" Naomi asked.

I nodded, glancing down at the baby swaddled close to her chest. His eyes were closed. "He woke you up?"

"He woke the whole room up." Moses' low laugh was like distant thunder. "Everyone except you. You're some sleeper."

"I was dreaming."

"What did you see?" Naomi asked.

"Gabriel was there. I think he gave me a glimpse of eternity, of the New Jerusalem."

"No dragon?"

"Not exactly. There was a storm behind me. I think it was sin and Don Cristo and evil. It sucked me away from the city and Gabriel."

"Did Gabriel say anything?" Moses asked.

"He told me to keep the faith and finish the race." I looked out to the east. The first touch of gray light filled the horizon. "And he told me I had one more day and one more night. I think the world might end tomorrow."

I turned to find Naomi and her dad gaping at me.

"It could be so," Moses said. "Bart thought the end would come this year. Zhang Tao has sensed we are close." His long face took on a sudden resolve—an exhausted runner ready to sprint across the finish line. "We don't have much time. We must make the most of it. Today we can prepare."

Naomi peeked down at her son. Her lips stretched into a smile. "Adam."

My breath caught. "You named him?"

She nodded. "His name is Adam."

"Anyone in your family named Adam?"

Moses smiled. "Only the father of all mankind."

"I'm ready," Naomi said. Her green eyes fixed on mine. "I'll go with you into Jerusalem. We're going to trust the Lord to return."

"Why the change of heart?"

"I received a word." She paused, as if savoring the memory. "As I drifted off to sleep last night, as I prayed, the Lord spoke to me: *Will I not protect the least of these?*"

"And what did he answer?"

"He didn't answer. He didn't have to—the question was all I needed."

"Why? What does it mean?"

"Who could be less than an infant? Especially an infant whose father has the spirit of the devil inside him." Naomi ran her hands along the baby's soft head. "God will protect Adam, no matter what the devil intends, no matter where I take him. I can't protect him. I can't save him. Only God can."

"So what do we do now?"

"We finalize our plan," Moses said.

We spent much of the morning talking with the others. Brie spoke on behalf of Chris. She said he wanted to attack now, while the technology was gone, to try to free some of those Don had captured. Zhang Tao encouraged everyone again to pray, to be thankful and hopeful. "How many souls might be saved before the end?" he asked. No one had an answer to that.

Around midday Brie let me join her to survey the perimeter. The sun was the only warm thing about the December day. The air was cool and the breeze carried scents of burnt destruction. The angels were nowhere to be seen. I asked Brie about it.

"They are messengers," she said. "After they finished their task of bringing you and Naomi here, maybe they went somewhere else."

"Like where? We need them for this battle. What I saw yesterday . . ." I took Laoth's advice and refused to let my mind dwell on the evil creatures. "The enemy has powers that only the angels can fight."

Brie nodded. "Some say the spiritual forces attract each other. The angels could be protecting us by staying away. We've managed to keep hidden so far."

"Is that your only plan?" I asked. "Just to hide here until Jesus comes again?"

"No." She gazed up the slope of the hill before us. "Just over there, Chris is gathering whatever forces he can. They will assault Don Cristo at the Dome of the Rock. His drones have had the entire old city on lockdown. Chris and his men have a few hideaways still, and a few tunnels like the one we used."

This sounded bad. "A direct assault might be a suicide mission."

"And?" She turned to me. "It's not suicide if the devil kills you. What choice is left? Chris would accept nothing but to go down fighting."

"It's a little surprising, he spent years pretending to be a watered-down, government-sponsored pastor. Now he's leading the fight, out in the open?"

"Which path takes greater courage?"

I didn't have an easy answer. "I guess they both do."

"It takes a man of immense strength and faith to hold true to his beliefs while walking the line of worldly acceptance. He's like a tightrope walker above a canyon, with no harness. You saw how he fell."

"He survived."

"He always has."

My mind went to a memory—her memory, which she had given me months ago in New York. "I've shared much of what you remember of him," I said. "I've remembered your love."

Her cheeks flushed, but I pressed on, thinking of Zhang Tao's story.

"You left out some important memories, though."

"Like what?" she asked, as if she knew where I was going.

"You gave me the time when you first met and the early years of your marriage. The joys, the challenges, and always the love. But you left out the engagement and the wedding. Why?"

"I gave you what you needed. Some things are still too personal. I hold them too close." She looked away from me, back toward the hill and Chris beyond it. Her finger twirled the tips of her blond hair. "We're all flawed," she said. "I'm selfish. I've always been selfish about Chris. He's mine, but he gives himself to everyone. It's who he is. It's the man I love. But the things that are just mine—" She lifted her hand and curled it into a fist. "Well, I hold those things tight. The day of our wedding was the best day of my life. It's just too much for me to share." She smiled at me. "You understand?"

I nodded, and it hurt. *Naomi*—a wedding day, the best day, a day we'd never have.

"You'll see Chris before I do, if Zhang Tao gets his way." Brie took my hand in hers and placed something in it. "Take this with you. If Don gets his system back online, it might be helpful."

I looked down at what she'd given me. A ring. A translucent ring of the order. "Whose was it?"

"It's Chris's. His and Zhang Tao's are the only ones we have left. It was for my protection, but he told me to give it to you if I saw you. I think he knew what was coming, parts of it, anyway. Bart told him it might come to this. Take the ring, give it to back Chris."

"I will."

"Thank you. Protect him, if you can. I know the end is coming, but I just want to see him one more time."

33

LATER THAT DAY, while the order was talking and praying in the hideout, two new people showed up. They both wore hooded cloaks. One of them strode through the door like he owned the place. He pulled back his hood, revealing a young face and long black hair pulled back into a knot.

"Riku!" Zhang Tao said, and they exchanged formal bows. "What news do you bring?"

"I've come from Tel Aviv. I learned more about Don Cristo's plan."

The other cloaked figure had already left, never entering the room. No one else seemed to notice. "Who was with you?" I asked.

Riku turned to the empty doorway, then back to me

with a curious expression. "I've come alone. No one followed me. Are you Elijah?"

I nodded.

"What did you see?" Zhang Tao asked me.

"Another person. Someone was with Riku, stood in the doorway a moment, then walked away."

"Perhaps one of God's messengers?" Zhang Tao said.

I eyed the doorway. "Maybe."

Zhang Tao smiled. "They continue to protect us. Come, let's all sit, share some tea, and hear what Riku has seen."

Moses served the tea while Riku began to tell us his story. I learned that he had previously served in the ISA in Japan. He couldn't have been much older than I. He talked about the technology Don had harnessed. "You ever wonder how he operates in so many places at once?" he asked, with his eyes on me.

I didn't need to guess. "His drones serve as his eyes and arms."

Riku shook his head, wearing a slight smirk. "That's only part of it. What do you think is behind the drones?"

"Demons." I shuddered at the memory. "I've felt something at work in them. Something dark."

"And how would spirit animate a machine?"

"Riku, just explain," Zhang Tao said.

Riku's eyes were amused as he stared at the wisened man. "Everyone says this Elijah kid is smart. Just wanted to see if it's true."

I kept my voice calm: "Don's adviser mentioned

superintelligence."

Riku nodded. "It's something like that. The ISA hadn't succeeded in its research, but Don did. Or was about to." He looked to Naomi. "But you already knew that."

A conflicted look crossed Naomi's face. "No, I mean, we all know Don has been developing powerful machines."

"What about Charles?" Riku pressed.

Charles. My friend. I'd last seen him at the Super Bowl, but it hadn't been him. Just his body. I looked to Naomi.

"The Captain suspected Don," she began. "There were whispers of UN superintelligence research. The drones had gotten stronger, faster, but they'd never crossed the threshold into their own creative ability. That kept humans in control. Don was pouring immense funds into breaking this barrier. It would have been a catastrophe."

Zhang Tao leaned forward and spoke. "The devil wanted to create a different kind of life. I believe the enemy has never liked God's creation—mankind." He paused. "How did you stop this?"

"ISA's main research center was in Shanghai," Riku said. "Naomi's group in ISA-7 had focused their surveillance there. But I found something near my home in Kyoto. My dad was a UN scientist. He let a few things slip that made me suspicious. He talked about *exciting discoveries* and *changing the world*—given his work with neurology and coding, I figured it meant something big. I tipped off Naomi."

"I told the Captain," Naomi said. "He never cared where we got our information. He assumed we'd report more freely that way. He just wanted to know, and he never ignored a lead. He called together a team. Four ISA-7 agents came by drone. Charles led us in person. We followed all the normal steps. Fake identity. Cleaning crew. Entry at night. We made it inside the underground lab without any alarm. Nothing about the lab was unusual. Stacks of hardware. Brain scanners. Coding stations. But then Charles synced with one of the stations." Her eyes closed, wincing at the memory. "I can still see his face. The terror, the disbelief. He told us we had to destroy the place immediately."

"What did he see?" I asked.

"I don't know. That's why I haven't brought it up. I never knew what he saw, or what it all meant. But we did what Charles said. The Captain ordered the lab's destruction. We set the explosives and fled. Before we could make it out the door, the place's security was somehow triggered. I still have no idea what happened. Something severed my sync. I was ejected from the drone, and next thing we knew, Don was using Charles's corpse against us."

"And that leads to what I've just discovered," Riku said. "I was in the ISA data center in Tel Aviv when the solar flare hit." He pulled a badge out of his coat pocket and smiled. "Cleaning crew, unit 23. I think it was the same kind of research center, except it was full of human brains. Androids were dissecting them, studying them, with guidance from human scientists. But these machines, they were also building organic bodies in large test tubes. They were twisting human DNA into something else. It wasn't—I don't know how to say it—it was . . . grotesque. The weight of evil is heavy in that place."

"What did the bodies look like?" Zhang Tao asked.

"They were made of metal *and* flesh. They had different shapes. Some with legs, some with wheels. Some with arms, some with guns. The androids were installing human brains in them, with spinal cords and everything. I think the combination of coding and biology, whatever it was, I think it was superintelligence."

"These must be the machines fighting for Don," I said, remembering Azazel. "They're more than drones."

Riku was nodding. "They had life. They were the devil's creation."

"How long has this been going on?" Zhang Tao asked.

"A few months, but the solar flare wiped them out. I traveled as fast I could to Jerusalem, running most of the way. I followed the order's trail of signs."

Zhang Tao stood slowly, stretching his legs and his back. He looked over our group. "What the devil attempts," he said, "the Lord will undo. Where evil takes grip, God sets us free. Surely the end is at hand. Let's pray for safety until then. Let's pray that sinners will be saved."

34

THE GROUP TALKED until the early evening. They spoke of the past month, of others they had lost. My mind drifted. Brie's words about Chris and Zhang Tao's story had sparked an unexpected conviction. I suddenly knew how to use my last day, to make it the best day. I had to ask Naomi to marry me.

My eyes settled on her. I watched her talking with her friends. I watched her face light up with love. Eventually she noticed me staring. She shrugged, smiled, frowned, made a funny face.

"What is it?" she finally asked.

A few others looked to her, then to me.

"Let's get some fresh air," I said.

"Why?"

I stood and walked to her. Moses held her son in his arms. He nodded for her to go ahead. I took her hand and we went down the stairs, heading outside. I didn't care what the others thought. I didn't care how crazy this was going to sound. We had only a short time left to live.

We found a small courtyard behind the apartment building. A burnt tree loomed over an empty and cracked fountain in the center. With no artificial lights around, stars flooded the night sky. The moon looked so swollen that it would burst.

I sat beside Naomi on a concrete bench. "Romantic spot, right?"

She smiled. "We've seen better. Remember that first night in DC, sitting and eating ice cream on the bench in Lafayette Park?"

"I'll never forget it."

"You've come a long way since then. You're better now."

Better. Without my precept. Without the ISA. Without my father. I didn't know what to say.

"I mean it," she continued. "That night—almost a year ago—you paraded around like a rooster trying to impress a hen."

"So you were impressed?"

She shook her head, her eyes playful. "Not at all, but I was curious. You weren't just any rooster. You were haunted."

"That's the look I was going for—haunted rooster."

She laughed. "You told me about your dream on that

bench. The first dream, with the dragon and St. Peter's. Did you bring me out here to tell me about another dream?"

I fumbled for the right words. I embraced the awkward. "You know how much you mean to me." I took her hand in mine. "You stole my breath the first time I saw you. You stole my mind the first time we synced. Remember?"

"That was after you whisked me away from DC to that fancy little inn in the country."

"When you were still playing games with me."

"Fair enough," she said, looking down at our hands. "The games ended in Rome."

"You were vulnerable after Don touched you. Nothing could have pulled me closer. I think it helped me grow stronger, too. In the desert. In Montana. In Geneva. I've grown every step of the way. That's the only reason I have the courage now to say this."

"What?" she asked, but I was already kneeling.

She gasped, her hand covering her mouth.

"Naomi, will you marry me?"

Tears filled her eyes. She tilted her head back and stared up at the stars. The moon cast the long lines of her neck in silvery light.

I was suddenly uncertain. "I know you weren't expecting this." I tried to explain. "I know it's a crazy time. The world is falling apart. The dev—"

"Stop," she said. "Just stop." She stood and pulled me to my feet. Her moist eyes were level with mine. "Yes."

"Yes?"

"Yes." Her lips pecked mine. "You are brilliant. We will celebrate, we will live and love. We'll get married, tonight!"

My heart raced. My mind still didn't believe it. "Tonight?"

She clasped her arms around my neck and kissed me again. Our lips parted. After a while—a minute, an eternity—she pulled back. She exhaled. "No reason to wait," she said, smiling wide.

We went together to tell the others. Most looked surprised, but not Brie, not Moses. They looked overjoyed, and like they expected it. Maybe I'd had that I'm-gonna-propose look on my face.

Everyone helped make quick arrangements for a ceremony. It was not quite what I'd expected for my wedding—a burnt-out apartment building with a few dozen guests and a little washstand serving as the podium. We didn't send invitations. We didn't plan an after-party. But we couldn't have been happier.

Zhang Tao officiated. Brie was the maid of honor. Moses was the best man. Naomi and I said our vows under the glow of emergency lights. Zhang Tao announced us as man and wife.

"What God has joined, let no man set asunder!"

Afterwards, Naomi led the group in song. She sang, *Be Thou My Vision*, and the beauty of it took me back to that first underground gathering in D.C. She'd entranced me then. I'd wanted her then. Now she was mine, and I was hers until death did us part.

Death was the last thing on my mind as Brie led us away. "We did the best we could," she said, opening a door several stories up in the building. The room spread the entire expanse of the building's top floor. The walls were bombed out. The floor was cracked and charred. But starting at our feet, a line of dimly glowing candles led to a bed in the center. They'd pushed two cots together and somehow found a mattress to go on top. Sheets draped down from the high ceiling, forming a white canopy.

"It's beautiful," Naomi said.

"It's all yours. We'll guard the stairs and maintain the watch around the perimeter." Brie smiled at us. "You two enjoy what still matters. If we lose love, we've lost the war." Happy tears filled her eyes as she stepped back toward the door. "Goodnight, Mr. and Mrs. Goldsmith."

After she left, it was just my wife and me. Naomi looked down at the threadbare dress someone had given her to wear. She was quiet, suddenly shy.

I scooped her into my arms, delighting in the feel of her.

She laughed. "Seriously?"

"Would you have it any other way?"

She smiled, shaking her head. "Take me away."

I carried her to the bed and laid her down gently on the sheets. I bent down to kiss her, but stopped. I remembered being in a place like this before.

"Is everything okay?" she asked.

I searched for the right words. "I need to tell you

something."

"You're not a virgin?"

"No, I mean, I am." I rubbed a hand through my hair awkwardly. "But in Babylon . . ."

"Yes?"

"It gives you whatever you most want."

"You wanted me?" she asked.

"Of course I did, and you were there." I looked around us, at the war-torn room. "It was different. The bed faced the ocean and the sand. But you looked a lot like you do now." I hesitated. "Perfect."

"What did you do?"

"I kissed you, but it wasn't you." It had been Jezebel, lust in bodily form. "Thankfully, something in me resisted. That's as far as it went."

"I'm glad," she said.

"Why?"

"Because this is real." She took my hand and pulled it to her waist. She kissed me lightly. "This is what God meant it to be. He created us for this."

Her words made Babylon vanish. Everything but her honey skin vanished. I kissed her deeply, and it was real, and it was better than I ever could've dreamed.

35

NAOMI AND I were up late. It was the kind of night that was supposed to go on forever—the beginning of a long life together of children and growing old. It was not the kind of night that was supposed to end with the lights flicking on before dawn.

But they did. The long fluorescent tubes along the ceiling blinked a few times, then blazed on with full yellow and buzzing light. They stretched the entire length of our empty floor. They cast our naked bodies in an unnatural glow.

I groaned at what this meant. "Don got the power on."

Naomi was already scrambling out of bed. She pulled the dress over her head. "He'll find us now. We have to get out." She reached down for a shoe, then paused. She grinned at me. "Husband, why are you just lying there?"

My head was still on the pillow, admiring my wife. "So what if he finds us? My life is complete."

"Good try, lover boy." She threw my shirt over my face. "Don's coming after us either way. We might as well go now. We can try to keep the attention away from here. Save a few lives."

"Fine," I grunted.

In a few minutes we were rushing down the stairs, to check in with the others. Everyone was rushing around with fear-filled, half-asleep eyes.

Moses found us and gave Naomi her son. "Adam," she said, smiling at him. I could have sworn he smiled back.

"You three have to leave," Moses said. "You'll ride out in the same truck. Your friend, Aisha, insists she's coming, too. We want to make it look like you were never here. As soon as the systems came back online, Brie got a message from Chris. He thinks we have about twenty minutes before Don's drones will be on us."

"What about you?" Naomi asked.

Moses pulled her into his long arms. "I'm sorry. Someone has to help protect our people. Pray for me. I'll pray for you." He released her and turned to me. "Protect her, son." I nodded, and he pulled me into an engulfing hug.

Naomi and I said a few other quick goodbyes, and then we were heading out. The truck was in the same place where it had dropped us off. Dumah was waiting behind the wheel. Gabriel was on top again. I peeked into the back and said hello to Laoth and Aisha. It was like we'd never even stopped. It was like nothing happened, even though the best night of my life had just happened.

We drove away from the building and toward Jerusalem. We rode along the main highway through chalk hills that grew steeper, tighter, with more buildings scattered throughout. As we crested the hill overlooking the city, the sun was cresting the horizon. But it was still dark. Smoke filled the air, casting everything in a surreal haze. The city's lights were still mostly off, except in the towers. Machines scurried up and down their sides, depositing human bodies again.

Up ahead the truck's headlights pointed to a tunnel. A few people watched us drive past. Their stupor seemed to have lifted. Their faces were frantic, afraid. A rock slammed into the windshield, cracking it. Other dull thuds hit the truck's sides. Dumah's iron grip on the steering wheel did not loosen. The tunnel gaped ahead, ready to swallow us.

"I don't like this." My voice was tight.

"We're following your vision," Naomi said. "And we're buying the order some time, if the drones focus on us instead." Naomi's eyes were locked on the tunnel. "But it looks pitch black in there. Should we go another way?"

God, show me the way, I prayed, but the plea rang hollow. It was eerily quiet, except for the rumbling truck engine. No word from God, no vision.

We rolled into the tunnel. The headlights did little to keep the darkness away, but they beamed onto a crowd of people before us. They crammed one side of the tunnel to the other. There was no way through, but Dumah didn't slow. He accelerated.

"What are you—" I began. And then I saw the shadows. Vaporous, shadowy wings rose from their backs. "Turn back!" I shouted.

A man in the center of the tunnel stepped forward. His eyes were black with red slits. He lifted his hand.

Dumah slammed the breaks. Too late.

The truck hit the demon's hand like a wall. We jerked forward. Seatbelts caught us. Adam started to cry.

"What's happening?" Naomi gasped.

"Demons—hundreds of them!"

Dumah slammed on the gas again, pedal to the floor, but we didn't move. The truck's wheels spun and screeched underneath us.

The demon opened his mouth to shout something, but Gabriel's sword stabbed into his throat. The demon fell back. Gabriel landed on top of him and raised his sword again. He faced the crowd of demons, alone.

They charged at him. More of the little kobolds swarmed up, swiping at his legs. The larger demons flailed at him with curved swords and whips.

I yanked off my seatbelt and reached for the door, but Dumah stopped me with his hand gripped around my arm.

"We have to help!" I shouted.

He was shaking his head. He pointed forward.

Laoth had come to Gabriel's side. The two of them stood back to back, fending off the hordes of demons.

Their swinging swords made arcs of light, but the darkness was overwhelming. A sword slashed into Laoth's side. She stumbled.

I looked to Dumah. "Gabriel and Laoth can't hold. We have to do something!"

Dumah glanced up. I followed his eyes and saw nothing but a dark ceiling above. He threw the truck in reverse and slammed the gas. We wheeled back so fast that I fell into the dash. Then Dumah slammed the brakes, knocking me back into the seat.

"Wait!" I shouted.

But he didn't. I clicked my seatbelt just before he threw it into drive and floored it again. We barreled ahead through the tunnel.

Rays of light suddenly beamed down before us and took form. Michael was among them. More angels had joined the fight, dividing the demons to the walls of the tunnel. The angels were outnumbered, a handful to hundreds, and not all the demons had moved by the time the truck reached the fight again. Dumah drove into the dark shapes with a *smack*. Bodies went flying and we broke through toward the other end of the tunnel.

"It's gone," Naomi said, her shocked eyes looking in the rearview mirror. "I saw the lights, but now they're gone. Were they angels? They're gone!"

I glanced in the mirror. There was no light to be seen.

"Oh God, no," Naomi breathed out. "What. Is. That?"

I looked ahead. In the center of the tunnel's opening, where the brilliant light of day shined in, a dark giant stood.

His skin was scaled like Jezebel's, and he seemed to swallow the light around him.

Dumah's hands clenched the wheel tighter. His foot did not relent on the pedal. But the giant raised his arm and the truck's wheels suddenly locked. We skidded and slid to the tunnel's opening, just feet away from him, just feet away from the morning light.

Dumah leapt out of the driver-side door, sword in hand. He raised it high, but the giant flicked his hand into the angel like a man flicking off a fly. Dumah's body flew to the side. He crashed into the far wall and did not rise.

The giant stepped to the side, and a smaller man was there. He approached us, smiling.

36

THE MAN STEPPED closer to our truck. "Alexi," I muttered.

"You know him?" Naomi asked.

I nodded, and he was there, climbing up the step beside the open driver-side door. He leaned in. "Elijah, Naomi, we're so glad you've come." He glanced into the dark tunnel behind us, then back into the truck. "Sorry about your friends back there. President Cristo said they were a threat. We had to take them out, but no worries. I'll drive you from here." He sat down behind the wheel and closed the door.

Alexi's insanity almost gave me calm, an odd sense of peace, like this was supposed to happen. "You're taking us to him?" I asked.

"Where else?" Alexi grinned and shifted into drive. We started rolling forward.

I placed my hand gently on Naomi's leg, trying to comfort her. She looked at me like I was crazy, too. She shook her head and mouthed: *No. Get out.* Then she opened the passenger door.

"I wouldn't do that," Alexi said.

Naomi was half way out, ready to jump, when she froze. A creature blocked her way. It was the giant that had thrown Dumah. Its red eyes fixed on her, and she cowered back into the truck.

The giant slammed the door shut and jumped up, its feet landing with a thud on the roof above us. Gabriel's spot. I hadn't heard anything from the back of the truck. Was Aisha still there?

The truck cruised out of the tunnel. Stretched out before us, appearing all at once, was the vast city of Jerusalem. Its hillsides were dotted with charred buildings. Smoke rose in hundreds of columns and gathered in dark clouds overhead. The resistance had left its mark, but still the towers had multiplied. They clustered around the center of the old city to our left, close to the immense golden dome. The dome might have been brilliant in the early morning light, but all its radiance was swallowed by the dragon perched on top of it.

Alexi started laughing. "Looks like a golden egg, don't you think?"

He still couldn't see it. The dragon.

"It looks like blasphemy, like evil," Naomi said. "Who

are you?"

"Is she always this harsh?" Alexi asked me, taking his eyes off the road. We were headed straight at a guard rail and a steep drop down the hillside.

"Look!" I pointed ahead.

Alexi turned and whipped the truck left, just grazing the rail with the left headlight. He cackled again.

"This is Alexi Marcos," I said to Naomi. "He is Don Cristo's political adviser. You've seen him before. He was the UN delegate who attended our first meeting at ISA. And he visited me in Don's palace. He was in the control tower."

Naomi studied me, looking confused. "Are you okay?" she whispered.

I nodded, trying to assure her with my eyes, then turned to Alexi. "Why does Don want us?"

We were winding down the hillside, to a valley leading up to the dome and the dragon. "Who knows," Alexi said, "but count yourselves lucky. See the line to visit with President Cristo?" He nodded up ahead.

An immense crowd covered the opposite hillside. They filled every inch of the roads weaving among the ancient buildings up to the Dome.

"Why do they want to see him?" Naomi asked.

"He is the world's best hope!" Alexi said. "It was true before the solar flare, and it's even more true now. Can you imagine the disorder and the destruction if Don weren't in control?"

"No," I said. "I can't." The buildings around us were

bombed-out crumbles. Faces ducked into alleys as we rode by.

"What do you expect?" Alexi shrugged. "Don had created a perfect world for mankind, but the enemy was jealous. He destroyed it. We will pick up the pieces. Don will bring Babylon back. He has sworn this to the people."

"What does he want with us?" Naomi asked.

"The same thing he wants from everyone: your allegiance to him." Alexi turned and glanced at the baby. "And, of course, his son."

The crowd grew thicker, and the roads grew tighter, as we approached the old city. The people parted for us, but we could still hardly fit. Some of them cried out for help and banged on the truck as we passed. I heard one or two shouts in Hebrew. Most were in Arabic.

The baby made a soft crying noise. Naomi cradled him close, but his eyes gazed out the front of the truck. His cries grew louder.

"Shhh, shh," Naomi said gently.

Another bang on the side of the truck, right outside Naomi's window. We hit a pothole in the road.

"Waa!" The baby whined. Then he was silent for a moment, winding up. "WAAAA!"

He wailed on, louder than I'd ever heard him. It made everything suddenly feel out of control.

"SHUT HIM UP," Alexi demanded, shaking his head in annoyance. He had his right hand over his ear, keeping his left hand on the wheel.

The baby's cries grew more intense, filling every space

in the truck's cab. It felt like we were sinking, the pressure rising.

Then Naomi started to sing. Over the baby's wailing, over the shouts outside and the truck's engine, her voice flowed like a soothing river. "*Be thou my vision, O Lord of my heart*," she sang, staring down at her son. His round, innocent eyes turned to her, and he quieted down. He let out a sigh—the kind of peaceful baby sound reserved for the voice of a mother.

"Thank you," Alexi said, still annoyed, "but could you sing something else?"

Naomi continued as if she hadn't heard him.

"No matter," he sighed, "we're here."

The truck stopped before a small gate in a huge wall. Two robotic guards stood on either side. A crowd of people gathered behind us. One of them shouted again in Arabic.

"Don awaits!" Alexi turned to me with a clown smile spread across his face.

Then a gunshot fired into the truck.

37

THE WINDSHIELD SPLATTERED in blood. Alexi's smile froze. His head fell forward and thudded against the steering wheel. There was no hair to hide the gruesome hole—shot from behind. I started to look back when the demon landed on the hood and glared inside. His red eyes matched the blood on the glass.

Naomi was pulling at my arm. I could see she was shouting, but I could barely hear her through the ringing in my ears.

I read her lips: "Come on!"

I shook my head, trying to wake up, but this was no dream. I stumbled out of the truck after Naomi. A crowd pressed around us. They all wore black robes, head to toe. Their bearded faces were a blur, and so were their voices, shouting in Arabic but muffled to my ears. A line of them had guns raised in the direction of the Dome, at the dragon. Before I could make sense of it, two of the men grabbed my arms. I barely resisted as they ushered me down the hill. We were heading away from the dragon, and Naomi was right in front of me.

We rushed down two old city blocks, then turned into an alley, then another. The crowd began to clear, and so did my mind. Someone had shot Alexi. Someone from behind.

"In here!" someone shouted.

The men corralled Naomi and me through a door. We left the alley and entered a plain room stuffed with more black-robed, bearded men. They circled tight around us. They blocked the door we'd come in through—the only door out.

Aisha was cradled in the arms of a man facing us. He set her down gently in a chair beside us. Aisha laid a gun down in her lap.

"You shot him," I said. It was neither a question nor an accusation. She'd been in the back of the truck.

She nodded. "I couldn't shoot the guy while he was driving. Too risky. But we stopped, and I heard Zafar's voice shouting. It was the best chance I was going to get."

"Zafar?" Naomi's eyes scanned the group around us.

The man who'd been holding Aisha took a step closer. "We are the Mahdi's people, what's left of them. He will rise again."

"This is one of the entrances to our headquarters

here," Aisha added. "The other leaders should be here soon, including one from your order."

"Who?" I thought of Chris.

Aisha shrugged, her lower body motionless on the chair. "I don't know. I've been here only as long as you have. When the power came back on a few hours ago, Zafar and the others picked up my signal. They knew we were coming into Jerusalem. They were waiting to save us from Cristo's men."

"*Dajjal.*" Zafar growled the name and glared down at the baby in Naomi's arms. "This is *his* child?"

"Yes." Aisha's eyes were sad. "I'm sorry, Naomi."

Naomi clutched her son tighter and stepped back. "He is *my* child."

"You are lucky," the man said. "I let you live. But not this . . . monster." Zafar nodded to the others in the room and shouted some order in Arabic.

Naomi crouched as the men closed on us. I tried to step in front of her, but the men were soldiers. One of them shoved me aside like I was nothing. A man reached for the baby, and Naomi shrieked and twisted away. She fell back and collapsed into Aisha. The men surrounded her, but then they froze. Naomi had Aisha's gun in her hand.

The men drew their own guns. At least a dozen of them.

"Naomi." Aisha's voice was calm. "Give them the baby."

"Never." Naomi held the gun steady.

"If you shoot, you die," Zafar said. "So does the monster."

"You know what *it* is," Aisha added. "The devil is its father. We cannot let it live."

Naomi shook her head. "The devil wants evil, but my baby is innocent."

"*Dajjal* won't stop until he has the child. Hand him over. Now."

I glanced at Naomi. Her eyes were fierce. I remembered my dream, with the baby in the dragon's belly. Maybe this was how it was supposed to happen. Maybe there was a compromise. "What if—"

"No more words," Zafar demanded, his eyes locked on Naomi. "Last chance, put down the gun."

He stepped forward, and Naomi leapt back. She swung her arm around and jammed the gun to Aisha's temple. "Try to take him, and Aisha dies."

"Take the child," Aisha said to Zafar. "I've done my part. I'm nothing without my legs."

Nobody moved. I slid between Naomi and the men.

"Easy, now," I said. "She'll shoot."

"Do it!" Aisha said behind me. "*Fire!*"

Zafar lurched forward. Naomi fired a shot.

CRACK.

The sound froze everyone, but only for a moment. One of the men slammed into me. We crashed to the floor. I tried to fight free, but another man grabbed my legs. They pinned me down, tied my wrists and ankles. Something was tied over my mouth. A bag went over my head.

Over the noise of men rushing past, I heard Naomi screaming, more shouting, and the baby wailing. Then, slicing through it all, I heard a familiar voice shouting, "*Stop. No, STOP!*"

EVERYTHING FELL QUIET, motionless. Through the bag over my head I heard heavy breathing from one of the men beside me, then Chris's calm voice further away.

"You're safe," he said. "Calm down, it's—"

"No!" Naomi shouted. "I will NOT calm down. They took my baby. They want to kill him!"

"The child must die," Zafar growled. "We have agreed."

Boots shuffled around me. I twisted on the ground, trying to get someone's attention, writhing as the cords cut into my wrists and ankles. I couldn't see, couldn't speak.

"Hold!" Chris ordered. "Hold. We did not agree to this. Akil is coming. Akil will decide."

Zafar said something I couldn't understand. The

movement stopped.

"We agreed the child was a danger," Chris said, "and that it would likely die. I never agreed *we* would kill it. Enough innocent blood is spilling."

"Innocent?" Zafar scoffed.

"All mankind is fallen, but this is a son of man, not of the devil. We have tested it."

"Your tests know nothing of the spirit, the *ro'eh*."

Roeh. My middle name, my mother's maiden name. I heard the shuffle of more movement, then a new voice. It had an Arabic accent, but it sounded older, wiser.

"All of you, sit."

No one protested. More movement—like chairs sliding across the floor.

"Zafar, hand the child back to his mother."

He grunted in protest, but then I heard Naomi's sigh of relief. She seemed to have forgotten completely about me. I tried twisting again, banging my arms against the floor. A boot slammed into my side with a dull thud. I lay still, gagged and hurting and listening in the dark.

"When the greatest evil arises, even enemies must unite against it." It was the old man's voice. Akil. I imagined him with a thick gray beard and a turban high on his head. "Chris and I have agreed in these last days. We cannot take the child if our partners do not consent. Chris?"

"We fight against Don Cristo," Chris said. "There is no trace of evil in this baby. The order, the Mahdi's people, and the true Israelis will make this last stand together."

"You made a deal with *them*?" Naomi's voice was

calmer, but I knew her, and her purity would not stand for this. "Do you know how many have died at the Mahdi's hands?"

"Quiet, girl," Zafar growled.

"Millions! That's how many have died because of *you*."

"Please, both of you," Chris said. "Naomi, they have protected me. Remember our call to love even our enemies."

"With limits!" Naomi gasped. "Do you love Don Cristo, the man who killed your children? Do you love the Mahdi, the man who bombed the innocent? Do you love the devil himself?"

A gunshot cracked into the air.

"Silence!" Zafar shouted. "No one says *Mahdi* in the same breath as *Dajjal*. Do it again and your friend dies, along with the child."

"Friend?" Chris asked. "Who?"

A shuffle of feet near me.

"Bring him here," Akil said. "Untie him."

Suddenly men were dragging me across the floor. Someone put me in a chair and cut the bindings on my wrists and feet. The bag lifted off my head.

The first thing I saw was Chris's shocked, smiling face. "I thought we'd lost you," he said.

Before me, standing tense around a table, were Chris, Naomi, Zafar, and four other men. One of them was older—gray beard but no turban. Everyone but Chris and Akil held a gun. I noticed Aisha, looking defeated, in a chair behind the others. Everyone's eyes were on me, but my gaze moved on, to a light, to a man sitting on the windowsill.

It was Gabriel.

"What do you see?" Naomi asked.

"*Gabriel*," I said, keeping my eyes on the angel. "You survived?"

He nodded. His eyes hinted at a smile on his flawless face. But he didn't speak. He didn't budge.

"So this is the seer?" Zafar said. "The boy with the visions?"

I ignored him. "Can you help us?" I asked the angel.

He held up his palms to me and mouthed the word, *Stay*. More words filled my mind. *Love your enemies. Give up what you hold tightest.*

"He speaks to the air," mocked one of the men. "We never should have partnered with these *Nasraneyin*."

I turned to the man who had spoken. His mouth was mostly hidden behind a long black beard, but it looked like a snarl.

"You cannot see what I can." I stepped forward, feeling a great energy rising in my core. "I have seen *Dajjal* in his true form. I have seen the Messiah. I have seen the end, and now I see the angel Gabriel." I turned back to the window. But Gabriel was gone. My mouth fell open as I faced the group at the table again.

The man scoffed, "I say we kill the baby *and* this lunatic." His face flickered, then was normal. I'd seen that before. On Gregory's face. On Vicente's.

"Demon." I pointed at him.

"You doubt me?" the man said to the others. "Listen to this *Yahoudy*."

"Quiet." Akil's voice commanded attention. "I had wondered . . ." The old man's eyes were fixed on me. They held wisdom and wonder and not a trace of fear. "We must have dignity, especially now. If our enemy drives us to this, he has won." He turned to the man whose face had changed. "Zafar, take Ifrit away. Lock him up. He is no longer one of us."

"What?" The man surged to his feet, but Zafar had already leveled a gun at him.

Zafar shrugged. "Akil's orders. Let's go."

"If not for your guardian," the man growled, glancing to the window and then glaring at me, "you would be dead now." But he did not resist as Zafar guided him away at gunpoint. Another man lifted a hatch on the floor, revealing stairs. They walked down them and out of sight.

Chris stood beside Akil, placing his hand on the man's shoulder. "We must hold whatever bonds remain. We cannot divide like this."

"What do you suggest?" Akil asked.

"I know what to do," I said. They all turned to me. "Your people want the child to die?"

Akil nodded. "Many wish this."

I turned to Naomi. *Trust me*, I tried to say with my eyes. "And we know you hold him close, he's your son. So we use him as a decoy."

"What are you doing?" Naomi whispered.

"We don't have much choice."

"A decoy," Akil mused. "Tell us more."

"Don Cristo wants the baby more than anything," I said. "We can use that to our advantage."

Chris was nodding. "We have our position near the Dome, hidden like before. So if we set the child somewhere out in the open, away from the Dome, Don's androids will come for it. They will bring a force, thinking we would defend that position. But instead we attack the Dome. One final onslaught, with all the firepower we have, against Don's headquarters."

"I like it," Akil said. "Zafar can lead our men."

"You can't take Adam from me." Naomi sounded uncertain.

"We won't," Chris said. "You stay with your son, as Don would expect. If we succeed, you might be safe for a while."

"I will call our forces," Akil said. "We will develop the plan. Let's meet again in an hour." He motioned for his men to leave. They stormed out of the room, but one of them stopped and lifted Aisha. Her legs dangled uselessly from his arms.

"Eli," Aisha said, "I believe you. I'll stay with you."

The man holding her looked to Akil, as if for permission.

"So it will be," Akil said. "But first, Aisha, let us take you to our people. This may be goodbye." Aisha nodded, and their group made its way down the stairs.

39

CHRIS, NAOMI, AND I sat alone around the table. Now that the bag was off my head and no one held a gun, I could take in the room. It looked ancient. The walls were pale, dusty stone, probably placed there a thousand years ago. The plain brown rug on the wood floor covered the stairs the Mahdi's men and Aisha had gone down, the stairs I felt sure led their way to Don.

"Tell me how you made it here," Chris said.

Naomi and I gave him the story. We described Don's palace, the fight in Tehran, and how the angels had brought us to the order. I told him what Brie had said. *I just want to see him one more time before it's over.* Then I gave him the ring.

"Thank you." His eyes were moist as he slipped it over his thumb. "I fear Brie and I won't see each other again.

But I feel her close. Our love gives me strength." He looked from me to Naomi. "As yours does. You'll need that for what lies ahead."

"And what's that?" Naomi asked, her voice quiet as she nursed her baby.

"I wish I knew," Chris said. "Elijah probably knows better than any of us. But here's what I know. We must have faith, now more than ever, in the darkest hour. We are going to suffer. Evil grows and crowds out the light."

"If faith is so important," I said, "why do you fight when others pray instead?"

"The body of Christ has many parts. I'm only a finger, pushing forward in his service. Others are the heart."

"Maybe I'm the womb," Naomi mused.

"You're more than that," Chris said. "You helped Elijah see and believe, and he has been the eyes. Elijah, why do you think Don wanted you to fight with him?"

"He said it was because of my ability, but I know that's not it. I think he wanted my visions, or maybe he didn't even know what he wanted." I paused, thinking of Chris's words. "I haven't done anything for these visions. I don't know why I have them, and I bet Don doesn't either. It frustrates him. He probably thinks I'm a prophet, a chosen one of God. Remember how the order said the devil wants to twist everything in God's plan?"

Chris nodded.

"Don thinks I'm part of that plan. Naomi, too, of course. He's been trying to get me on his side."

"He has ways to do that against your will," Chris said.

"I know." I shuddered at the memory of Azazel in my thoughts, and of my feelings at the sight of Jezebel. "Don has tried. He has done it, for a time at least. I'm still flawed."

"Praise God for the solar flare," Naomi said. She was patting the baby on the back, burping him. "Don might have seized Elijah's mind if not for that. His demons can somehow work inside the machines. The lines between spirit and matter are weakening."

"Then we must pray for help," Chris said. "Tell me more about these angels who helped you. How many have you seen?"

"Hundreds."

Naomi nodded. "They're fighting Don's demons. Some look human. Some I can't see at all. But Elijah can."

"I see only what God shows me. I've seen the spiritual forces collide, and our side is not always winning. Demons overwhelmed the angels who brought us into the city. If not for Aisha shooting Alexi, we'd be in Don's hands right now."

"Some of the Muslim people have proven themselves to be allies," Chris said. "Akil is a wise man, a good man. Your friend Aisha is sharp. Zafar, hard as he is, saved my life a few days ago. This battle has many layers. Good and evil are sifting, separating. Old lines are fracturing. New ones are forming. We'll attack, but it won't go well. Not even the angels can prevail without the Lord's return."

"Then why attack Don?" Naomi asked.

Chris shook his head, but his mouth was drawn tight,

determined. "I've said it before. No one knows for sure what to do in these days. Many believers went into hiding. They have been hunted down and killed. Others have fought. They have been killed. What can we do but follow the Spirit's leading? Prayer is my greatest weapon, but I must do something with my body. I will not sit idly."

"But you and Zhang Tao are the last of the leaders who live," I said. "Don wants to kill you."

"Do you suggest I hide?" Chris challenged. "No place is safe. I must do everything I can to fight him."

"You cannot charge recklessly into death," Naomi said.

"*Reckless?*" Chris asked, his voice rising. "He destroyed everything I had. He killed my children. Next he will try to kill my wife and me, and both of you. Do not judge me as reckless for fighting evil." He rose to his feet, and his eyes settled on me. "I soldier on until the Lord returns. What about you Elijah?"

Stay, Gabriel had said. If Naomi was going to be on a rooftop with her child, that's where I was going to be. "Naomi and I will stay together." I rose beside her.

"I understand." Chris motioned for us to draw closer. "You must follow His lead. Let's pray together before I go."

Naomi and I went to him, and he put his arms around us. I put my arm over Naomi. Then Chris prayed. The words were a blessing, a plea for protection, but they felt like a goodbye.

40

AN HOUR LATER Aisha, Naomi, the baby, and I sat together on the roof of the old city building. The sound of war surrounded us—gunshots, shouts, and the metallic rumbling of machines. Most of the conflict came from the hill above us, the heart of Jerusalem. I had a clear view of the dragon on the Dome. The creature's body was motionless, while its head swiveled and surveyed the city around it. Several times the dragon's red eyes passed over us, but it did not stir.

"Why doesn't he cry more?" Aisha asked, eyeing the baby skeptically. "Through all these things, I've heard him cry only a few times. It's weird."

"He's special." Naomi rocked the child slowly in her arms. "Sometimes I think he senses more than we can. It could be—"

"Look." I pointed to the dragon. It had unfurled its wings. Bigger than I remembered. The whole city seemed to fall under their shadow.

"The dragon?" Naomi asked.

I nodded. They still couldn't see. "It's been still, but the wings are moving, like it's ready to fly."

Aisha's eyes locked on the Dome. "What else is happening?"

"You see the robots repairing the towers?"

"Yes."

"And what's around them?"

Aisha studied the sky. "There's smoke everywhere. It makes the sky dark and gray."

"Do you see the smoke swirling?"

Aisha shook her head. "What do you mean?"

"Within the smoke and clouds there are thousands of threads of black swirling around."

"I don't see that."

"Some of it's in shapes, like shadows of winged creatures . . . like ravens. And woven through it all is the dragon's spirit, black threads extending and crossing in every direction."

Aisha was staring at me. "How do you sleep?"

"It depends on the dream," I said. "All that darkness and black and evil can't compare to the light I've seen."

"You mean the angels?"

"No, they're as bright as all this is dark." I motioned to the sky and over the city. "They're in balance, but the man

I saw, Jesus, is different. When I remember him, I forget the darkness. It's as if none of the darkness, none of the evil, even exists compared to him."

"But what you see now sounds horrible."

"It is, but it will pass. The light won't. It—"

Gunshots fired out rapidly, close to the dragon. Thin trails of soaring missiles zipped past overhead, straight at the Dome. The dragon draped its wings around it, forming a black wall.

BOOM!

Missiles exploded against the wall. The force of it rippled through the sky, shaking the rooftop where we sat. Smoke billowed out, obscuring the dragon, covering us in a pale mist.

We pressed closer together. We didn't speak. Aisha was trembling. Naomi's hand found mine, held it tight. For a moment, everything fell silent.

The smoke made it harder to breathe. I coughed. The baby did, too. It whimpered lightly.

Aisha held her sleeve over her mouth. "Did the attack work?"

I shook my head uncertainly, but as the smoke began to dissipate, I knew the answer was no. I knew it because a pair of giant red eyes appeared through the smoke, right beside us.

I started to shout, but before a sound left my mouth, something slammed into my body, knocking me back hard. An instant later Aisha crashed down beside me. I sprang to my feet, wincing and holding my chest. I rushed to where

Naomi and Adam were.

But the dragon had them in its onyx claws.

"Elijah!" Naomi shouted, her face frantically searching for the creature that held her. Her arms wrapped tight around the baby at her chest, protecting him.

I started to charge for her, but the dragon's face emerged again through the smoke. It froze me where I stood. Petrified. With a victorious snarl, the creature leapt off the building and flew away. It disappeared into the smoke. And just like that, Naomi was gone.

I fell to my knees in desperation. Smoke stung my eyes. Tears streamed down my face. I was supposed to protect her, to be with her through the end. Losing Naomi wasn't in my dreams. This wasn't what the angel showed me.

I cried out to God. I raised my arms, pleading.

I began to hear words in the wind, in my mind. *You are a failure. Elijah, the prophet, the seer, the failure.*

I shook my head, trying to make the words stop. They didn't.

God is not coming. He is not coming. You are a failure.

The dark and powerful words wrapped around me and became true. I could not deny them. It was my fault. I was the one who could see the dragon, and I didn't even mutter a warning. I'd set this up and watched it happen.

Well done, prophet. Well done, seer. You have always served me.

I felt a hand on my back. I turned and saw Aisha's face through the blur of tears.

"Was that . . . the dragon?" she asked.

I nodded and pointed to the Dome. "The devil has

them now."

She propped up on her elbows and gazed at the Dome. She turned back at me with hard eyes. "What are we waiting for? We have to go there."

Her words were like a slap across my face—in a good way. No use staying here, no use mourning. Despair and failure were the devil's weapons. God was still with me. So was my friend, Aisha. I took a deep breath, steadied myself. I wiped away tears. "Let's do it."

"I know which path Zafar and the others took. It's a tunnel. I can show you the way." She glanced down at her paralyzed legs. "Can you carry me?"

I knelt down and pulled her body into my arms. I rose slowly, steadying myself to balance her weight. Her slender frame was not heavy, but my legs were still unsteady after the dragon's attack. My chest still burned with pain. Bruised ribs, I guessed.

She smiled up at me. "I'm glad we still have each other. I always knew you were something special. I think part of me always hoped . . ."

The look in her almond eyes caught me off guard. "Aisha, I—"

She put a finger over my lips, then moved her hand to my cheek. "I know, Elijah. I know. You don't have to say anything." She broke our stare and looked to the side. "It's that way. Down the stairs."

I moved toward the stairs. "You're right. I'm glad we still have each other."

She nodded. "Now let's go get Naomi."

41

I CARRIED AISHA off the roof, down the stairs, through the abandoned building, and into the room with the hidden hatch. We descended more stairs and reached a dark, stone-walled tunnel.

I scanned both directions. "Which way?"

"Right." Aisha pointed. "It'll be hard to see, but the floor is smooth. I'll tell you where to turn."

I began the way she'd pointed. In a dozen steps the pale light of the stairwell behind us was gone. My steps blurred into a rhythm of dull thuds. We seemed to be heading uphill. The darkness invited a flood of feelings about what had happened: terror about the dragon and Naomi; doubt about whether we could do anything now; awkwardness about what Aisha had said; weariness from the weight of her body; warmth from the closeness of her; coldness from the empty tunnel; and, glowing underneath all that, a smoldering ember of faith and hope. I believed Jesus was who he said he was, and that kept the ember burning, my feet marching.

"That way," Aisha said. An open doorway lay ahead of us, on the left. "We're almost under the Dome now."

My arms and legs were aching as I turned to the left, down another dark tunnel. But light was ahead. "And take this right," Aisha directed.

After a few more steps I rounded the corner. We entered a larger room, a cavern. I'd hardly taken in the surroundings when a beam of light flashed over my face, leaving my eyes no time to adjust. I staggered back.

"Eli," whispered a man. "Thought I'd never see you again."

"Jacob?" My uncle. Maybe the last of my family alive.

"It's me," he said, lowering the flashlight. He wore military fatigues and a helmet. Dark hollows sank beneath his eyes as he glanced down at Aisha. "Zafar said you'd stayed back with the other girl and the baby. You were supposed to be our cover."

"The dragon came. It took them. Don must have them now."

"Cristo has everyone." Jacob pointed up to the ceiling. I could see better now—a ladder led up through a shaft in the carved-out stone. "We're staging our final assault," he continued. "We'd be a lot stronger if you'd sent some funds, like I asked."

"What do you mean?" But the memory came to me—what he'd said the week of my Dad's funeral. *Our city is Jerusalem, and it could use your help.* "I've had my own troubles getting here. I don't think I could've been much help."

"Your troubles *are* our troubles." Jacob was shaking his head. "Now you've given Cristo everything. You've done nothing for us."

"That's ridiculous," I said. "I gave him nothing. I've fought him in every way I can."

"Oh? How's that?"

"I—" I'd stayed in his palace. I'd fought inside his drone. Against my will, but still. "I've prayed for God's help."

"Some help." Jacob raised a rifle. "This is how you fight against a tyrant. I've signaled to the others that you're here, that our cover's blown. They'll be here any second. You keep *praying.*" He cocked the gun with a snap. "I'll lead the true fighters out of here. I'll scrape and claw my way to range, and I'll put a bullet in Cristo's head."

Good luck. I held my tongue, kept my face blank. Then I did what he said: I prayed. *God, give me wisdom.* This wasn't in my dream's script. I had no idea what to do, but the last thing I wanted was to forget my hope. *Please, give me peace.*

A group entered the room from behind Jacob. Chris pressed through to the front of the mismatched troop. Zafar was at his side.

"Glad you made it," Jacob welcomed.

Chris ignored him and looked to me, then behind me. "What happened? Where's Naomi?"

"The dragon has her."

Chris closed his eyes and breathed out heavily. A moment passed in silence, then Chris turned to Jacob. "We have no choice left. We'll attack as you and Zafar wanted, but my men aren't facing Don without Elijah."

"He's no soldier. He'd rather pray than fight."

"Elijah sees what we cannot," Chris replied. "We are not all meant to fight the same way. He'll help us now."

"So says the Christian," Jacob mocked. "So say the people who have never had their land—their heritage—face centuries of assault after assault. We've had to fight with our backs to the wall since before your religion was born. You can never understand what it means to fight."

"You are a soft people," Zafar agreed. "This is why only our lands have stood against Dajjal."

"But our lands are lost!" Aisha shouted. The men gaped at her in my arms, as if surprised the paralyzed girl would command their attention. "Tehran is destroyed," she continued. "The Mahdi is dead. Cristo is here, reigning over the city we all call holy. We can't fight him as we've fought before. We must fight him as Elijah does, with faith, with—"

"Silence!" Zafar shouted. "Your words are nothing, girl. Soft lands, soft people have corrupted you." He spat on the ground and turned to the other men. "The Mahdi disappeared and reappeared once. He will again. He and Isa will defeat Dajjal. We fight until that day. We fight until victory!"

"My people share this duty," Jacob said, facing the men

with him. "We fight for Israel until the Messiah comes."

"The Messiah *has* come," I said. "I have seen Him. He has spoken to me."

Jacob jerked toward me and grabbed my arm. Our eyes locked. "You help Cristo, and now you abandon your heritage?"

"You don't understand," I said, my voice calm, my soul calm. Words flooded out of my lips, as if born outside my mind: "My faith has been completed. It was empty before, now it's full. I will speak God's truth to the world. I will seal Abaddon's fate. The Lord has spoken, and I am the messenger."

Jacob released his grip and gaped at me. "What's wrong with you?" He sounded exhausted and confused. "What would Arella think of you now, Eli?"

Arella. Mom. "I know what she thinks. I have seen her, and she has spoken to me. She gave me a message for you."

Jacob shook his head gravely. "Your mind is lost."

"She said it was Jesus who caught the roof above your daughter."

Jacob's mouth fell open. "Wh—who told you this?"

"My Mom prayed over your daughter. She told me, *it was the Messiah who caught the roof above his daughter.* He knew you needed her in these last days."

"I . . . there's no way you could know this." Jacob was shaking his head. The other men were staring at him with confused looks as my uncle's eyes grew moist. "What have you become, Elijah?"

"They say he's a prophet," Zafar scoffed.

"He is *the* prophet," Chris said. "He is Elijah come again."

The words sank into me. "I am only a servant, a messenger."

Jacob eyed me, uncertain. I held his stare in silence. He breathed out heavily and looked away, facing the other men. "If Chris would have Elijah fight, I won't stop him. We need every weapon we have."

"Thank you," I said.

Jacob nodded to me and straightened his back—all soldier. "The time has come. Follow me."

42

THE MEN BEGAN climbing a ladder through the narrow shaft above. Jacob was the first to reach the top, before I'd even started going up. He slid open a manhole-sized lid, revealing the smokey sky above.

Most of the men had crawled out when Chris paused at the foot of the ladder. He clasped my shoulder. "We'll try to get Naomi back, okay?"

I nodded. "And then we'll get Brie."

He smiled like it was an inside joke. We both knew the odds. "And if not today," he said, "maybe tomorrow—after the Lord's victory." With that he started up the ladder.

I knelt down beside Aisha, where she'd been sitting. Her arms reached around me, holding onto my back as I rose and began to climb. The sounds of fighting grew louder with each rung. As we neared the opening, I heard gunshots, confused shouts, cries of pain, of death.

"Sure you want to go?" I rested a few rungs shy of the top. I couldn't see anything but dark sky above.

"Is there any other way?" Aisha asked softly.

"Yes, we could stay in the tunnel, hide. These men won't survive against Don and his machines, and we'll go down with them. You won't even be able to run."

Her grip tightened around my shoulders. "Did I need my legs when I shot Alexi?"

"I guess not."

"Then I will fight. Perhaps I can do more. I want the honor of dying to defend what I love."

I nodded. She was right. Death no longer mattered. We could run for a little while, but it would come back to this. There was nowhere left to hide, and no reason to try.

"Why are you still waiting?" Aisha asked.

"I'm worried about what might happen after you die."

She laughed lightly. "I'm not. I've watched you, Eli. I share your belief in the light, and maybe even in *Isa*. I believe we will meet again on the other side."

The way she said it, with such hope, made some of the tension slip out of my shoulders. "He came to me, Aisha. I saw him and heard him. Jesus, *Isa*—he's everything."

She studied me, her eyes concentrated. "I'm beginning to understand." The sound of a gunshot pulled her gaze up. "Let's go now."

As I climbed the final few rungs up, I felt the warmth of hope and faith and peace. I felt God was with us, like maybe we could serve him in this fight. I felt like we could even win.

But then I felt a hard, cold fist. The instant I peeked out of the hole, something grabbed me and lifted us out.

A demon's charred face was in mine. "He knew you'd come," it growled. "He's waiting for you."

The demon tore Aisha off my back and threw her to the ground. Then it slung me over its shoulder and charged toward the Dome of the Rock. Androids flanked us. I looked back and my breath froze. The huge space was packed with androids in ordered lines, while dark blurs of spirits danced and weaved in their midst.

I twisted to look where we were going just as the Dome's huge doors swung open. The smell of smoke and incense filled my nose. The demon flung me forward. I hit the ground, rolled and slid against something firm. Legs.

Don stood over me, black suit, open arms, and grinning as always. "Welcome, Elijah! It's so nice to have you back. You're in time to see my strength fully restored."

My gaze moved past him. His presence felt almost familiar compared to what surrounded us. Pale yellow light lit the cavernous round room. Thousands of colorful tiles covered the floor. They probably covered the walls and the ceiling, too, but I couldn't see them, because stacks of oval chambers crammed into the space. Each chamber sat on top of another, knitted together by fibrous cables running from the floor to the ceiling.

The ceiling was a swirling chaos of black and roiling flames. I could see the dragon's eyes staring down at us through the blackness, as if the Dome's golden ceiling weren't even there. Dark wisps flowed out of the dragon, out of the darkness, and into the chambers along the wall. It seemed like the dragon was pumping evil into the entire hive—the chambers and whatever they held.

I took a deep breath and gagged. The incense was masking a heavy smell of sulfur. I wiped sweat off my forehead. My body shook and sagged, weak as if I had a raging fever. I felt clammy, nauseous.

Don backed away and stood between two columns along the Dome's inner ring. At the base of the columns were two empty chambers. "These two are for you."

"Who?" I asked. *Lord, help me. Help—*

"You and Naomi, of course." Don pointed past one of the chambers, and I saw Naomi's motionless body sprawled on the ground. "I keep my promises," Don said, but I was already scrambling, running to her.

I put my hand to her neck. She was breathing, she was alive. *God, you brought her back to me once. Don't let her die now. Please God. Please God. Pl—*

"You brought her to me." Don's words severed my prayer. "And now she is yours. She made for a fine Mary, don't you think? Actually, the mother of my enemy was not nearly as beautiful. Mary was meek as a mouse, just like her pathetic child. Naomi is a true woman clothed with the sun. I'll keep you both around, and you may continue to worship our son forever. I have new bodies prepared for both of you."

Naomi had begun to stir. Her green eyes opened.

"Elijah."

"I'm here."

"Where's my son?" Her eyes scanned the room.

"He's in his chamber." Don pointed to a capsule near the center of the room. "He's growing into what he was meant to be."

Naomi lurched forward, but an android grabbed her. Her eyes blazed at Don. "God alone gives life."

"Oh, I don't deny he started this mess on earth. He's also the one who abandoned it, who would let it destroy itself. I'm the one who will preserve it." He stepped to the chamber closest to us and ran his fingers along its smooth surface. "Souls will no longer die," he mused. "They will remain in constant pleasure, transported from one body to another, and I will draw on their energy to enable this perpetual, blissful life."

"I'd rather die." Naomi cringed away, but the android wouldn't let her budge.

"You never cease to amuse me." Don stepped closer to us. "Still thinking you have a choice."

I tried to move back, but another android seized me. Its four arms clamped around my arms and legs. I didn't bother thrashing. I prayed, *Thank you for letting me see Naomi again.* I smiled at her. "The Lord will return."

She nodded and closed her eyes. "Thank you, God, for giving us this life. Thank you for loving us. Thank you for Elijah. Thank—"

"Enough," Don said. Naomi's mouth slammed shut. He glared at her. "You won't think it either."

The android holding Naomi suddenly injected something into her neck. In a breath she fell limp in its arms. It hauled her toward the chamber.

Don turned to me. "Last chance, Elijah."

"You said we have no choice."

"She has no choice, but you still do. Your soul is salvageable. You're not fully turned. Not yet."

God, what can I do? I felt helpless. I prayed with all I had.

The sound of voices made me turn. A group of androids carried tied-up men, one by one, through the Dome's doors. The first machine reached Don and dangled a limp man before him.

"Christopher Max." Don smiled, then pointed to a chamber half way up one of the Dome's walls. "That one."

The android moved to the wall and climbed up it like a spider. It deposited Chris's body into the chamber. Translucent fibers closed over him. A dark tentacle plunged in, as if stabbing into his heart.

Another machine approached. "Zafar al-Saud." Don pointed to another chamber. "That one."

The android holding him rushed away.

And so it went, name after name. They passed in seconds, but Don paused when Aisha was presented to him. She writhed in the machine's arms. But it did nothing.

Don put his hand to his chin. "This pretty one was supposed to die with the Mahdi, but I'll keep her. She'll make a good trophy."

Aisha opened her mouth as if to shout, but no words came. Her red face was shaking furiously.

"Hold her to the side for now," Don commanded, and more androids holding men filed through. Most were unconscious, but a few flailed like Aisha. It didn't matter—each one found himself in a chamber, pierced by the dragon's spirit.

When they were all gone, Don turned back to me. His black eyes burned. "What's your choice?"

I felt the universe compressing around me. All the darkness and evil and power were here, in Don's command. "Why me?"

"Because you've served me well, Elijah."

"You're a liar."

Don laughed. "The best there is. And so are you. Don't you know the enemy called you from before the creation of this world? You were meant to be like your forerunner, like Elijah the Prophet. You were meant to serve the enemy. He gave you the gift of sight. He planted the seeds of greatness in you, and what have you done with it? *You* brought the virgin to me in Rome. *You* showed me the places where the order hid. *You* put the Captain in my hands in Geneva."

"No!" I shouted. But I couldn't think, couldn't pray.

"*You* joined Azazel, fought with me in war. *You* helped kill the Mahdi. *You* returned with my son. What more could I ask?"

"No, no." I stammered. "That's not—"

His words battered into me again. "Why else would I honor you now? Why else would I want you beside me? You are highly gifted of God's creations, and you have served me. Well done, my faithful servant."

"You're a liar," I said, but was it true? The android released me, and I fell to my knees. I tried to remember, tried to see the light, the white throne. *God, I'm here. You must be here. You never fail, you never leave. I'm sorry for how I've failed. Forgive me, please. Show me truth.*

YOU ARE MINE. Jesus—His words, more like a sword than a voice.

I surged to my feet, unable to suppress a smile. Don stepped back.

TELL HIM YOU WILL SPEAK FOR HIM.

"I will speak for you."

Don blinked in surprise. Then he looked over his shoulder. A bowl-shaped helmet was there, like the one I had used weeks ago in Don's tower in Geneva. This bowl was made entirely of black fibers, where the other had been translucent.

It all made sense. God wanted me here. He wanted me to speak to the world. "I will speak for you," I repeated.

Don turned back to me, and his lips turned slowly into a smile. "Yes, yes Elijah, you will." He paused. "Reboot your precept."

Fear struck me. With my precept on, wouldn't he control me? Prayers rose up and bubbled over inside of me. An unexpected word slipped from my lips: "*Hosanna.*"

"What was that?" Don asked.

I kept my face blank.

"Your maker stopped listening long ago, Eli." He stepped closer, his beautiful face sneering down at me. "I told you. This world is mine now. The angels are fighting a battle they'll lose, because their god is not coming this time. If anyone would sense him coming, it would be me. If you try to say anything against me, you will watch Naomi suffer before she dies."

"Okay," I swallowed.

"Good." He pressed his fingers to my temples. "Turn on your precept. Now."

"V . . . reboot."

43

INFORMATION HIT ME like an avalanche. With my precept on, my mind churned at twice the speed. I saw more. I heard more. And, most important, I *felt* Naomi. Her precept was on—maybe forced on—but either way, our sync was there. The data told me she was slipping back into consciousness from whatever the android had injected.

"Excellent," Don said. "It's time to address the world."

I hesitated. He sounded so sure. Was this really what the Lord wanted from me? *Jesus, how can I speak, when he is in my precept? How—?*

"You underestimated me," Don said. "I told you, he's not listening. Nothing, no one, can stop me now." His gaze locked onto me. This time he wasn't smiling. He was concentrating.

A command entered my precept: *Come here.* The words were Don's, unspoken and impossible to resist.

I stepped forward. Another step. The bowl-shaped helmet hung before me, dangling from the Dome and the dragon above.

Another command: *Put it on.*

My hands lifted to the helmet's sides. I couldn't stop. I tried to speak, tried to pray. Don's presence crowded out everything else. My arms shook violently, fighting back, resisting.

Don's words slammed into my mind: *I don't care what you believe, Eli. Didn't any of the order tell you that? I care only about what you do, and this time, you will obey me.*

He lifted his hand and tapped his fingers in the air. I looked in horror as my hand mirrored his. I was nothing but the puppet, my precept the strings, and Don the master.

GOD! I shouted inside. My inner voice sounded small, weak, distant.

Don answered: *You will say what I say. Think only what I allow you to think. Connect now.*

And then I was lowering the bowl over my head. I was feeling it push and prod against my skull.

A shot rang out, the sound close but muted. I saw a hole appear in Don's forehead. I saw him fall back. I saw a man slam into him. But all of that was minuscule, because I was watching it through an ocean. It was the ocean of minds in the universe, just as I'd seen it in the UN tower, in the Omega project.

This was different, though. I didn't need to enter one of the pinpricks of light, as I had when I'd spoken to one person. I could shout to them all at once, and I knew they would hear, because the liquid streams of black connected me to them. It was all black except for their tiny lights and the blazing fire of my soul.

SPEAK, ELIJAH.

Don's voice was gone. These words came to me from deeper than myself. Words of history before the creation of the world, revealed once, and now revealed again. They came out of my lips easily. They were what I was born to say, and every living soul was going to hear.

"*Behold,*" I began, "*the day is coming, burning like an oven, when all the arrogant and all evildoers will be stubble.*" In the ocean before my eyes, millions of pinpricks of light opened, like flowers opening for the sun. "*The day that is here shall set you ablaze, says the Lord of hosts, so that it will leave you neither root nor branch. But for you who fear the Lord's name, the name of Jesus Christ, the sun of righteousness shall rise with healing in its wings. You shall go out leaping like calves from the stall. And you shall tread down the wicked, for they will be ashes under the soles of your feet, on the day when I act, says the Lord of hosts. Heed my words, for I am Elijah the prophet before the great and awesome day of the Lord comes.*"

I finished, and all at once the universe was gone. I was back in the Dome. I'd been yanked out from under the bowl.

Don glared down at me. The hole in the center of his forehead was like a third eye, dripping blood. I felt nothing but contempt for him. My eyes looked past him, to Jacob's body on the ground, to the gun just outside his outstretched arm, and then to the figures assaulting the dragon above.

The angels had joined the battle.

I recognized one of them—Michael. He raised his sword. It was not of the world. It was the same as the dragon's flame, light against dark. They slammed into each other.

"Look at me," Don demanded, and I did.

His face was astonished, terrified, and small. Yet his presence filled my precept again. He was holding back nothing. He couldn't hurt me, I knew, no matter what he did. I had touched the Word, and the Word would conquer.

Don glared at me. "You chose wrong, prophet."

His fist closed around my throat. He lifted me without effort, and my feet dangled above the ground. I didn't fight back, didn't struggle, didn't speak. I didn't have to. I had done my part.

With a sudden fling, Don hurled my body through the air, through the Dome's giant doors, and into the open square. I crashed onto the ground and lost my breath. I clung to consciousness as my body rolled and finally slid to a stop.

My back was against the ground. I couldn't feel anything below my waist. I tried to rise up, and fell. My right arm was broken. I twisted my head to the other side and saw paradise.

Naomi.

She was lying only feet away, as motionless as I was. It was like that moment in the ISA hallway almost a year ago, except now her ashen, freckled face was alive with energy. She smiled, as if I'd done the right thing.

"I heard you," she said. "Elijah the prophet. You finished the race."

I smiled back and tried to say something, anything. The effort nearly made me pass out. Nothing could move up my throat, where Don had crushed it in his grip. Each breath hurt, halting and irregular. So I just lay there, broken but staring into Naomi's eyes, listening to the roar of battling angels and demons, light and dark.

Thank you, Lord. Thank you for this final moment.

Something beyond Naomi caught my attention.

The sun.

It was low in the sky, grazing the top edge of the wall around the square. The day's light was fading, just as surely as my life was.

But the sun seemed to grow. I'd never seen it so big.

"I see them now, the angels," Naomi whispered by my side. "Paul taught that it would end this way: *The Lord Jesus is revealed from heaven with his mighty angels in flaming fire.*" She paused. "And Peter wrote, *The heavens and earth that now exist are stored up for fire, being kept until the day of judgment and destruction of the ungodly.*"

I blinked my eyes shut, and when I opened them again, the sun was twice its size, maybe three times. It almost filled the sky. It was all I could see.

My face felt heat. More heat.

Hotter. Burning.

Then, all at once, as if bursting like a swollen red balloon, the sun exploded.

That's how I got to this moment.

44

I'VE LOST MY sense of time. I feel heat all around me. The sun no longer fills the sky. The sun *is* the sky—molten flames washing over me and over the earth.

My skin starts to burn.

But I'm still breathing, still thinking, as if watching the pain from outside myself. I try to shake the burning sensation away, but it's only getting hotter. It's searing my flesh. My skin reddens and cracks and blisters. I'm boiling over, all my emotions and energy screaming in pain, only no sound can leave my mouth. It is bone dry, burned out.

Then something cool touches me. I look to my side—a distant memory tells me Naomi was there, on the ground, in a different place. But this is a familiar man, the one who came to Patmos, who saved Naomi.

"Elijah," he says. "It is well."

His voice is cold water. It is relief, but only for a moment. The heat pulls me up into the flattening, burning red sun. Now the heat scorches me inside. Again I'm outside myself, watching as I fall to my knees, as my body melts away.

"Elijah."

I look at the man. Brown hair, brown beard, lightning eyes. He takes my face—I must have a new face—in his hands and smiles. Such strong hands. They feel cool.

"I am with you," the man says.

Then we'll both burn! I'm thinking.

"Not if I am in you," the man answers.

Then a voice fills the air: "I AM the Alpha and the Omega, the beginning and the end. It is done."

This voice calms me. It's deeper than the ocean, and no fire can burn while those words resound. "Watch," the man says, "the first things have passed away. My Father is making all things new."

The exploded, melting sun has puddled into a flat expanse, like a universe collapsed into two dimensions, into a lake of fire. This lake stretches farther than I can see, and somehow I know it doesn't end, it has no bottom.

I suddenly realize I'm standing on something that's not the lake, and I'm not alone. I'm in a crowd. There are more people than I can count around me. I can't look at the people, but I know they're there. They know I'm here. We are countless, but we are nothing compared to the burning lake.

From the space above, the blackness of outer space, dotted with a million stars, something darker than black appears. It starts as a dot but grows larger and takes form. It is the dragon, soaring down. No, not soaring. It is falling, as if hurled toward the fire. Its wings flap helplessly. There is no wind for them to catch. Its legs flail. Its neck snaps around like a snake's as it spins and plummets down.

Then I see a man rising out of the flat, burning expanse. He is below us, and he is enormous—I'm an ant watching this giant. His arms are reaching up, and buildings and machines are in his hands, like tiny little toys. Flames from the lake lap at his chest, smoke rises from his flesh. His face is twisted in agony, but it's a face I know: Don Cristo, Dajjal, the devil. Everything that was beautiful about him makes me hurt inside. It is the pain of losing what could have been.

The dragon streams down like a comet, flashing past me and slamming straight into Don, plunging them both down into the lake. Red-hot fire splashes over them, waves ripple out, and an immense smell of rot and decay fills the air. Then the lake is smooth fire again.

I feel a gentle breeze on my skin. I hear a faint trumpet. The awful smell is gone as I look up. From where the dragon had appeared, in the distant void, a bright dot of light glows. It approaches me, beckons me. As it comes closer, it takes shape as an immense throne. It is whiter than snow, and so is the robe of the man seated on it.

My feet lift off from wherever I stood. The breeze is now a gusting wind, whipping at my hair, bringing tears of joy to my eyes. The moment the throne and the man are level with me, everything else is gone. The ground, the lake of fire, the stars—they have fled away. Space and time are gone.

But the others are still with me. *All* the others. I know, beyond doubt, that this crowd holds every human soul that has ever existed. This gathering completes humanity, but we are not finished.

The end of our first journey comes now, in judgment. This certainty proceeds from the throne before us. The great white throne with God upon it. He is like an inverse black hole—a consciousness of infinite gravity but brilliantly light instead of dark inside at His core.

I feel an irresistible draw toward His light. I race at it, faster and faster, until I'm facing the throne. Now it's just me. Somehow the others are gone.

"He has believed in me," Jesus says, stepping between the throne and me. "He comes through me."

My being unfurls with all its memories and deeds, as if they're exposed on the open page of a book before me. For the first time I see the black spots, the sins, without any concealment. Before I can shrink back or try to speak, the sins begin to fade. The light consumes them. The page is blank. Everything is light.

"Now the book of life," Jesus says, and another book opens before me. Every word in the book is a name, and I can see nothing else. I have no breath, no desire, except that I'll see my name written within these pages.

45

"ELIJAH ROEH GOLDSMITH."

My name is written in fine black script on the white page. I'm in the book. Right here. Right now. I see it, I see me, and immense feelings of relief and hope and joy sweep over me.

"Welcome." It's Jesus's voice. He's smiling at me. The throne no longer sits behind him.

"Where are we?" I ask.

"Eternity, Elijah. Come, you will see."

He puts his arm over my shoulder, and he points forward. All I see is white. It's so bright, I can barely hold my eyes open. "But I can't see anything."

"You will, you will." He gives me an encouraging nudge at the back. "Step into the light. I will see you inside."

I step forward. I feel like I'm moving through a mirror, passing into a different universe, and suddenly I'm standing in front of an immense wall, clear as glass. A round gate stands before me, and so does an angel I recognize— Gabriel.

"Welcome, Elijah. Would you like to see more?"

I nod, and he takes my hand. We are suddenly on a mountain, as if we just shifted in place. The crystal wall and the gate are far below, with a city stretching as far as I can see into the distance.

"How did you do that?" I ask.

His patient eyes rest on me. "Our bodies are not bound by space here. You can be anywhere you want."

I don't understand, but I want to try it. I imagine myself down in front of the gate again. I envision myself shifting again. But I'm still on the mountain. My feet haven't budged. "It's not working."

He points to the mountain under our feet. "You *want* to be on this mountain now."

It's not a question. He is right. This is where I want to be in this moment, on the mountain, able to see everything.

"Desire is pure in eternity," Gabriel says. "It is pure because it has no conflict. In Babylon, Lucifer would have ruined what God created to be good, using sin to hold you captive to your desires. But here God reigns, not sin, and we have the fullness of joy and pleasures forevermore."

"Can I control my desires?"

Gabriel smiles. "Of course. Your desires are your own.

But your life before this place shapes what you are here. The greatest saints in the fallen earth have the greatest desires here."

"What does that mean for me?" His words make me curious—do some have it better than others? How can that be perfect?

"The Father created each of us with a capacity, like an upper limit. But in the fallen earth, he enabled everyone to push that limit as far as possible in the mold of his son. The further a person pushed, the greater his capacity grew. But now and forever, everyone's capacity is fully reached, and no one can know anyone else's capacity. This means we all live in our fullest potential, our deepest satisfaction, our most conceivable joy."

I nod, agreeing, feeling as if I lack nothing.

"It is paradise of the soul." Gabriel sweeps his arm out to the city below. "So, now you stand where you want, in your fullest potential in this moment, and what do you see?"

I gaze out over the endless city. The word "city" doesn't fit. This is an entire world laid out below, only it has taken the form of buildings and streets. They are made of light and gold, glass and steel, water and tree. "It is the most beautiful place I have ever seen. What is it?"

"Some say it is the New Jerusalem. Others say it's the City of God." Gabriel closes his eyes and breathes in, then out, like he's inhaling a joy even he can't contain. His eyes open in a blaze. "I call it home."

"How far does it go? How many people live here?"

"This takes time to understand," he says. "Do you remember the dimensions of your country in the old earth?"

"Yes." All those memories are there, but they are bland and dim compared to this.

"The city where you once lived, New York. Do you know how far it was from, say, Florida?"

"A very long way. Maybe a thousand miles?"

He nods. "This city has four perfectly equal sides. Each one is about that distance."

I'm trying to wrap my mind around this, but the angel continues. "It's a poor comparison, though. Places on the old earth were flat."

"And what's this?" I look out at the city again. It has buildings and so it is rises into the air, but the ground beneath it is flat.

"Are you ready for the full view?" Gabriel's voice hints at a great secret.

"I guess so."

"Do you *want* it?"

My thoughts reach up like a prayer, and they wrap around a desire. This desire is to see the full city, to understand its magnitude. I decide this must be a little of what Gabriel meant by desire being pure. "I want to see it all."

Gabriel takes my hand. "Then you will."

My feet do not move, but my vision does. The city seems to pivot and rotate, revealing a whole dimension I had missed. It expands, too, filling the space above and below. I cannot see its edges or its top or bottom. My mouth falls open.

"You see," Gabriel says, "it is as high as it is wide. This is the new heaven and the new earth."

It seems impossible, but I remember that people once thought the earth was flat. I feel like Galileo and those early discoverers whose minds first grasped that the old earth was a sphere, not a disc. This city is a cube, not a square. The crystal wall around it is like a perfect glass case. But I'm still confused. "Where is this mountain we stand on?" I ask. "How does it exist outside the city, if the city is everything?"

"We have more dimensions here," Gabriel says. "We are standing in one of them, and the layers—the height of the city—are in it. With God at our center, we wrap around his presence in these layers. These mountains and the space beyond, they are the remote layers."

I think for the first time to turn around. Behind me, stretching as far as I can see, is the most stunning landscape I have ever seen. Beyond the rocky mountains where I stand there are great bodies of water, dense forests, and flat deserts. The swirl of colors is overwhelming. The waters are the bluest blues, the trees are the greenest greens. "How far does it go?" I ask.

"It goes forever," Gabriel says. "At the farthest reaches, in the cold stars beyond, the distance from God's center is the greatest. There, at that point of greatest separation, the heavens fold back on themselves and return to God. This is the meaning of infinity. It has no end. It loops back. Everything returns to God. In the center."

I focus on one of these cold stars in the distance. It's another planet. "Do people live out there?"

"Some do for a time. You may travel as far and as long as you like. But it is our nature to return to God. Even the animals tend to stay close."

"The animals?"

"Yes, and far more than you will have known on earth. They are His creations, too."

I feel an urge to turn back to the city. It helps me understand what Gabriel means. I want to explore, but I never want to lose the sight and feel of this purest of lights emanating from the city. "Can we go inside now?"

"If you want it, then you know how."

"Will you come with me?"

"As far as the gate," Gabriel says. "I return to my post."

I nod. This time I take Gabriel's hand. I want to be in front of the gate again. I *want* it, and so it is. I *shift* with Gabriel and we are there.

46

I SAY GOODBYE to Gabriel and walk through the gate. I'm on a long, straight road. I look down and pause. I cannot help but kneel and stare. Tiles the size of fingernails fit together in perfect patterns. A bright gold octagon is fitted against eight amber triangles. Lines of fiery orange circles spray out from there, melded between the softest yellow mortar. I could stare at these tiles for hours, but I remember I want to see the city. I rise to my feet and keep walking.

Now I look ahead. In the distance, the buildings grow taller and taller. They almost seem to form a tunnel, and at the end of the road is a light like the sun. It is warm on my face. It pulls me forward. My steps feel light and free.

I'm passing homes made of perfect white stone blocks.

Their doors and windows are standing wide open. The smell of baking bread drifts from them. I hear the sound of a symphony.

A man is bent over a lawn of grass in front of one of the homes. He holds scissors in his hands. He is trimming the grass with the care of a stylist. Not a blade of grass looks taller than any other. I would call the color vivid, but words are not enough. This green would make emeralds jealous.

"What are you doing?" I ask the man.

He looks up at me, smiling.

"Bart?" I stammer. His face is so young, but his eyes are unmistakable.

"One and the same," he says. "I have waited with great expectation to see you, Elijah. How was your journey?"

"Good. Miraculous." I look again at the scissors in his hands. "What are you doing?"

"Some of this day's work."

"Cutting grass?"

He nods.

"Don't you get bored?"

"Not at all. I do this because I love it. Have you ever seen a more magnificent lawn?"

I shake my head. "It's impressive."

Bart stands and breathes in deeply, with a pride of workmanship. "I love the soft feeling of the grass between my fingers. I love the smell after each cut."

"I'm allergic to grass."

He laughs. "Not here. Well, I doubt it anyway."

"What else do you do here?"

"Many things. I'm first cello in a local choir. I also govern this district."

"Govern it?"

He nods. "I'm like the mayor."

"Interesting," I say, unsure what it means to be a grass-cutting mayor here. In fact, I'm surprised by how little I know of this place. It doesn't bother me. My mind is free and clear. There's no static, no confusion, but there's so much to learn. It's thrilling, like the first page of a book. "I have a lot of questions."

"We have a lot of time." He puts his hand at my back. "Won't you come in to eat? You can ask me whatever you like."

I hesitate. I'm not hungry, and I was supposed to explore the city.

"You've just arrived," he says, "I know how that feels. We are all new here, but I at least had a little time in the old heaven. Some things are similar."

"The old heaven?"

"Yes, follow me, we will talk more."

I nod and walk with him into the home. The moment I step inside, I'm flooded with a feeling of warmth and brightness. Maybe it's the smell of freshly baked bread, or the lush stringed music I hear. To my right is an office. It almost reminds me of Bart's cramped space under the Cathedral in Washington, though that place seems far away. This office has many papers and books in neat stacks. There is no skull on the desk.

"I still read a lot," Bart says. "Come, let's eat."

He leads me down the hall. The next room on the left has a broad wooden table with six chairs. Two sets of plates and cups and silverware are there.

Bart motions for me to sit. Then he calls out, "Evelyn?"

Moments later a woman enters the room. She is wiping her hands on her apron. "A guest!" she says as she spots me. She is short, with round shoulders and a bun of dark hair. The spark in her eyes makes me think she's a ball of energy as much as she's a person. "Welcome, what's your name?"

"This is my friend Elijah," Bart answers. "I told you he would come." He puts his hand gently on the woman's shoulder. It is a familiar touch, the way a man touches a woman he's lived with for decades. "Please, sit," he says to her. "Let me get another setting. The bread smells ready."

She nods. "Thank you."

As Bart bustles out, she sits in the chair beside mine, curling up her legs to sit on them. I sense that she always has some bounce to her movements. She smiles at me. "You have questions."

"I don't know where to begin."

"It is always important to know where to begin," she says. "You see, the beginning is the same as the end—God. He's at our center now, and he always will be." She takes a sip of water and sighs.

"Who are you?" I ask.

"Oh dear!" She puts her hand over her mouth.

"Pardon my manners. My name is Evelyn Holland. Sometimes I forget we don't all know each other yet. That will take care of itself in time."

"I thought time didn't exist here."

She laughs. "Bart always said you could see to the truth of matters. You're quite right, in one sense. Before, on the old earth, time had an unrelenting pace and a limit for each of us. I would know—I reached my limit, I died. Now there are no limits. The pace cannot be judged. Existence moves, as does time. But time's movements are of little significance in the face of eternity. You can divide anything by infinity and come to zero."

I take a sip from my glass. The water tastes pure and cool. *One billion divided by infinity equals zero.* The math works. But it doesn't explain much. "What did you mean by 'the old earth'?"

"The earth where we once lived," she answers. "It was—" she pauses as Bart returns. "Dear, would you care to explain?" She looks from him to me again. "You probably already know Bart's the bookish type. He thinks often about such things."

"Evelyn knows more than she cares to admit." Bart sets down a tray and begins laying out a spread of steaming loaves, butter, and jam. It smells better than a Parisian baker's shop at dawn. "But then, so do you Elijah. You were there to see the old earth's end. I'd love to hear you describe it. We saw it only from a distance."

I try to find words, but none do it justice. "It was very hot."

Bart laughs. "Still making me drag out answers, I see. Well, I imagine it was hot, and probably loud, too. Peter said, *the heavens will pass away with a roar, and the heavenly bodies will be burned up and dissolved, and the earth and the works that are done on it will be exposed.*" He pauses. "So was it the sun?"

I nod. "I think it exploded, maybe started a chain reaction. There was so much heat, like all the stars melted into a lake of fire."

"That must have been something to see," Evelyn says, holding out a loaf. "Here, have some bread."

I take the loaf and set in on my plate. My body feels no ache of hunger, despite the amazing smell. I'm staring down at the bread. My mouth is watering. My stomach is full.

"Not feeling hungry?" Evelyn asks. "Welcome to the new earth. There is no hunger here."

"How does that work?"

"You have a stomach," Bart explains, "but like the rest of your body, it's perfected. Hunger was a symptom of brokenness, of emptiness. Everything is full here. We eat for the joy of it, and for fellowship. There was a reason our Lord taught us to break bread together. May I bless the food?"

"Okay."

Bart closes his eyes and holds out his hands. Evelyn takes one of his hands in hers, so I do the same. My eyes close. Bart prays, in a patient and measured voice, "Our present God, be with us now, dine with us, fill us with your holy light." He speaks for a while, thanking God. The words deepen my relaxed happiness.

When I open my eyes, a familiar man is sitting with us at the table.

47

I'M STARING AT the man. I've seen him before. I saw him just before I came to this place. "Jesus?"

"Welcome, Elijah." He holds out an open-lidded jar. "Here, try this with the bread. Evelyn's jam is wonderful."

"Thank you!" Evelyn says.

I nod, speechless. I take the jar and spread some of the dark purple jam on my bread. Jesus takes a bite, and so do I. The taste is more than a taste. It is a sensation of immense joy. I'm eating bread with God. I can't get my mind around this.

Jesus picks up a pitcher of wine. "Would you like a drink?"

"Yes, thank you."

He fills my glass, then Bart's, then Evelyn's, then his.

"A toast!" Bart says, raising his glass.

"A toast," Jesus replies. "To our Father's glory."

We clink glasses and drink. The rich red liquid satisfies more desire than I knew I had. It's like I'll never need to drink again.

"This is part of my Father's creation," Jesus says. "Every good and perfect thing is from Him." He studies me, smiling. His eyes are halos of light. His face is a royal welcome. "You have many questions. What do you want to know?"

Everyone imagines this moment. I get to ask him a question, anything I want, but only one word comes to me. It's too simple. It's too big. I ask it: "Why?"

"A wise question," he says. "Human thoughts, human words—they can never answer this question. But I am the Word, the Way, the Truth, and the Life. I can show you the answer."

"Will you?"

He looks to Bart and Evelyn. They are beaming up at him.

"You'll come again soon?" Evelyn asks.

"Whenever you want, call on my name." He rises from the chair. His movements are fluid and easy, as if nothing could ever resist his motion. He holds out his hand to me. "Come, follow me."

I stand and take his hand.

And we shift.

We're somewhere new. There's an immense tree above us, bigger than any oak. The ground under my bare feet is soft, green moss. A stream gurgles to my right. The sound of children laughing comes from a stone cottage to my left.

"You are showing me why?" I ask, and he knows what I mean. I want to know why God did it. Why make the earth, why create the humans, and why pick me?

"Yes, I'll introduce you to my beloved friend. He enjoys answering these questions. He has a word for it. In the written Word, the Spirit breathed out all the answers that humans could grasp. The answers are a story, of course." He walks toward the cottage, and I fall into step with him. "Now the story continues, and you may understand more, as much as your spirit allows."

My spirit? The Spirit? I ponder this as I follow the Lord's stride. I've never felt happier walking from one place to another. My legs are flawless, fast. Our movements are in unison.

We reach the wooden door and he knocks.

"I'm going now, but I'm always with you," he says, and then his body vanishes before my eyes. He is gone, but he isn't. I still feel him with me, like he is everywhere. I realize he'd let me walk beside him because I'd wanted that. Now I just want to know what's behind this door.

The door opens.

"Elijah!" Brie rushes out and catches me up in a tight embrace. Chris follows right after her and sweeps both of us into his arms.

"Come, come!" Chris says. "We just got here, too. We're about to have a reading."

"A reading?"

But they're already whisking me into the cottage. We walk through the orderly little home and out the back door. There's a ring of thick stumps overlooking a vast range of mountains. Seven people are sitting around the circle.

I know Chris, Brie, and another man. "Patrick?"

His athletic frame rises, even stronger than I remembered. He looks me up and down with his bright blue eyes. They look a little older but a lot wiser, a lot happier. "You've aged well, my friend." He's laughing warmly, and I realize I don't know what I look like.

Brie escorts me forward. There's a basin of still water in the center of the circle. "Take a look," she says.

I look down and see my face. The eyes are the same, except brighter. Everything else is a little different. I look stronger, fuller. My hair is curly and long, brushing my broad shoulders. I look older than I was on earth, but not old at all. What I remember of myself before is like a flat, two-dimensional mask, and this is four dimensions— timeless.

"Our bodies here reflect our souls at their best," Chris says. "Some bodies are older or larger. Some are younger or smaller. We're each where we are most comfortable, and we can change, we will change. Looks like you start around thirty."

"I'm nine!" says a boy in the circle. I know him, too. He's Chris and Brie's son, Toph, now a few years older. "I can still beat Patrick in a race."

Patrick gives him a friendly shove. "When I let you."

"That's what you think." Toph is laughing. He

stretches his arms high in the sky. "Last one to the tree's a rotten egg." He's already running around the corner of the cottage, and Patrick leaps up and chases after him. A blond man and a blond boy, sprinting as if nothing else mattered but their motions, as if their race were worship of the highest order.

"Joy comes in many forms," says a woman's voice. I turn and see her. She's standing in the door of the cottage, smiling at me.

I could never mistake her almond eyes. "Aisha."

She rushes forward and hugs me. "I heard Jesus brought you here. I couldn't wait to come."

"But how are you *here*?" I say, and I realize that could be an awkward thing to say, but no one seems to mind.

She puts her hand to my cheek. "The Lord used you to save me. I was all pride. I thought the Mahdi and I could save the world. I thought we could defeat the enemy."

"What happened?"

"When I was at my most broken, after the crash, after I lost my legs . . ." She looks down and bends her legs, as if to remind herself that they are whole and perfect. "You came with the angels and fought for me. I still don't fully understand why, but it chipped away the darkness and let the first light shine through."

"The first light?"

She nods. "When you climbed out of that tunnel with me in Jerusalem, you were fearless. Not like a soldier bravely going into battle, but like a man who believed without doubt that the battle would be won. I knew the fight was over when one of the machines grabbed me, but I remembered your faith and its source. I called out to Jesus then, and He was there, with me at the end."

"That's amazing." I shake my head, struggling to accept that my pitiful example had helped her, especially when I was the one who had so needed help. I think of my question again: *why?* "Jesus brought me here. He told me he'd show me why."

"And so he will," says a man who is sitting on one of the stumps. He holds out his arms in welcome. He has a thick brown beard and neatly cut brown hair.

"Who are you?" I ask.

"A citizen of this kingdom, like all of you. I've lived in this cottage and many other places. Sometimes I clean clothes for my neighbors. Sometimes I wash their feet. I study the stars, too. In all this, I serve the Lord."

"What's your name?"

"John."

48

THE MAN NAMED JOHN urges our group to sit in a circle. He's standing facing us and the cottage, with mountain ranges behind him. He looks like he knows everything there is to know, but he's not the old John from Patmos, at least not the one I met.

"You were with the Lord on earth?" asks Chris.

"I was." John's voice is warm. "All of you were. He was always there."

"But you could feel him, touch him!" Brie says.

John nods. "I wish everyone could have seen him as I did. No one could have doubted. But of course, that's not how God planned it. Even many who saw his son during his life on earth had clouded eyes. The enemy used many tricks, but that is over now. Jesus had to die for us, so that we could know him, so that we could be here."

"Why?" The question boils out of me again.

"We're all new to this forever place, but I've been in his presence for ages. I understand more of it now, though we'll always be getting closer. Each step forward will make our lives sweeter. It's eternal progress. It's eternal joy."

He pauses, as Toph and Patrick race back around the cottage. They're not even breathing heavily as they sit. I realize the crowd has grown. I didn't notice the others come. There are dozens of faces around us. One of them I know: my uncle, Jacob, only he looks even younger than Toph. He doesn't see me yet. He is grinning with boyish innocence, intent on John's words.

"All of you, watch," John says, "and you will understand."

He lifts a white towel and steps forward to the basin of water. He dips the towel into the water, and as he does, a gorgeous light begins to emit from him. The light flows in waves like living threads. It swirls around John. His hands holding the towel are glowing.

He bends down in front of Toph, the little boy, and he begins to wash his feet. After the race with Patrick, Toph's toes and heels are dusted in dirt. But as John rubs the towel over them, the light swirls around and into and through Toph. The boy holds out his arms, marveling as the warm and brilliant threads wrap around him.

"The Lord abides in me," John says. "He abides in all of us. What was unseen is now seen." He holds the towel out to Toph. It shows no sign of dirt. "Now you."

The boy takes the towel and dips it into the water. He goes to Patrick and washes his feet. The light is dancing around the three of them.

John has another towel. He kneels in front of me and begins washing my feet.

I watch in awe as the light ebbs and flows around my legs, my waist, my chest. It goes through my chest, out my back, and I can feel it. The feeling is strong and pure, like one of those brief, fragile moments on the old earth when existence made sense—and it was good. Only now, that feeling isn't going away. It's deepening and wrapping around me.

John finishes and holds the towel to me. "Sin is gone. The law is fulfilled. We abide in his love. We see the Comforter, the Spirit of truth which proceeds from the Father."

I feel weightless as I stand. I dip the towel into the water. I feel brighter than the sun, and I want to share this brilliance. I turn to Aisha and the threads of light spread from me to her. We understand each other now as we never have. She is my sister. We have the same love. We both abide in it.

I wash her feet, and so it goes.

In the end, it's not our feet that matter. It's the light we've shared, and the sharing gives glory to the light and to its source. It is glory to the Father. It is what we were made to do, to serve and love each other for the beauty that God made in each of us.

I look around at the smiling faces and, for the first

time, I realize I want to see a face that is not there. I remember her name. It is from so long ago, but it is still bright in my mind: Naomi.

John comes to me. Maybe he senses my unmet desire, because it is so out of place. "Elijah, what do you want?"

"Where is Naomi?"

John turns to Chris. "He is ready. Will you take him to Elijah?"

Elijah? I don't understand, but Chris nods and leads me away. We don't say goodbyes. We don't need to, because the infinite circles always lead back, away, and back again.

As I follow Chris, I'm fascinated by what John said, that I'll live in a place here. And it must be where Naomi is. "Who is Elijah?" I ask. "Is he going to take me to Naomi?"

Chris pauses. We are under the great tree again. "I will show you, but you should remember, there is no marriage here."

I remember Evelyn and Bart, and Brie. She was beside Chris, just like she was on the old earth. "What about Brie?"

Chris smiles. "My love, my soulmate. What we have here is better than marriage. We share God's glory like the angels. My bond with Brie is deeper, richer. We are all one, but some souls still gravitate toward each other."

"I want to see Naomi."

"You will. The first Elijah meets us here. He will take you."

"The first—?"

Before I finish my question, a man appears beside us.

He's wearing a robe whiter than white. His face glows like the sun. It's not Jesus, but it looks like a man who has soaked in light for lifetimes.

"I am Elijah." He holds out his hand to me.

"Me too." I shake his hand and the glowing threads of Spirit wind around us. Chris waves to me and walks away.

"I know," says this other Elijah. "We are of the same mold. I was one of the few to see into things as you did in the old earth."

"You're the prophet?"

"Yes, as you are." He pauses. "Ready?"

"I think so. Where are we going?"

"Before I show you," he says, "you should know this is not the forever place. The whole city, this whole creation, is the forever place. You, me, everyone—we will move as time passes. We have room to grow. There may be times when our souls crave the city's beating center, nearest to the light. There may be times when we desire solitude, in the farthest reaches of the universe. Eternity ebbs and flows."

I understand this, at least pieces of it. "So how do we know when to move, and how do we acquire a new place? Do we purchase homes, like on the old earth?"

"No. Think of it, how could anyone own what God alone created? And here, how could currency exist where all are completely satisfied?"

"I see."

"God made you to see." Elijah smiles. "The workings of eternity's perpetual motion remain beyond our vision, but what we can understand is balance. God created us to live in balance. When you desire a cottage in a forest, someone living in that cottage will desire something else. The places open as you are led to them."

"It seems too—" I struggle for the word, and an old, small idea arises from my memory. "Too utopian."

"Utopia is an idol, a myth that could never exist outside God's will. Perfection is possible only in God's new earth, within his will."

I don't answer. I'm still puzzling over his words.

"We will have eternity to consider how this works," Elijah adds. "You will know much more as soon as you come to the throne. First, you should see your home. Others will want to join you when you go before the throne."

"Like Naomi?"

He nods. "She is there. Ready?"

"Yes."

He clasps my shoulder and we shift. We're standing on a street of gold. To the side is a river of glistening water. Around us are towering buildings. Everything is bright, reflecting the light that shines ahead of us. It's more dazzling than the sun, but I don't have to shield my eyes. I want to bask in its warmth.

"Would you like a drink?" Elijah's eyes are fixed on the river.

Yes. I'm already walking toward the river. Elijah bends down on its bank, and I do the same. We dip our hands into the water. It's cool, refreshing. I lift it to my lips. As the drops enter my mouth and slide down my throat, I feel pulsating energy, like that of a thousand lives filling me. The current is electric but without shock—my body conducts the energy and delights in the sensation.

"The river of life." Elijah rises to his feet. "Reminding us, through the Spirit, that we will never die. Come."

We walk down the golden road. Birds soar overhead. A breeze caresses my skin. I still taste the water. I still taste life, bubbling up inside me. It's another one of those perfect moments on the old earth, the kind I tried to hold tightly, but that slipped through my hands all the same. This moment isn't slipping. It has the feeling of permanence.

Ahead is an immense tree. It towers as high as the buildings, with the column of light behind it. The branches drape overhead, weighed down by the largest fruit I've ever seen.

Elijah turns into a building. He pauses in the door, waiting for me. "Naomi is inside."

49

BEFORE I FOLLOW Elijah through the door, I crane my neck back to see the building towering above. Its vertical lines merge into one in the distant sky, like a line stretching beyond my understanding.

"Step inside," Elijah says, "and you'll be taken to your floor."

"Aren't you coming?"

He shakes his head. "I'll wait here for you. Go on," he encourages, "you'll see why."

I enter and find myself in a cavernous glass room. There are no other doors, no decorations. But the pattern of the floor is different in the center. I walk to it and gaze down at the fine lines forming stars. Then the floor begins to rise under my feet, lifting like an elevator. It goes up faster and faster. Now I'm soaring.

As the floor slows and stops, I see a number: 875. Is that what story I'm on? I look up. The glass shaft I've been rising in keeps going up. I'm maybe halfway to the top. Four openings are in front of me, each with names above them. The names, like the number, are written in light on steel. The words are in different languages, but I understand them all. One of names is Elijah Roeh Goldsmith.

I step through the doorway under my name. The hallway sparkles as if covered in diamond dust. As I move forward, mesmerized, the hall curves to the left and opens into a room with a gleaming white floor and high ceiling. The far side of the room is entirely open. No wall, no glass. It ends with a ledge and a thin golden rail. A woman leans on the rail, looking out over the city.

I approach, my eyes fixed on her. For some reason, I count my steps. It steadies my movements, stills my thoughts. One, two, three, four—farther than it looked. I count seventy-three when I arrive at the woman's side. By now I'm certain it's Naomi.

She turns to me, beaming. She looks just like she did the day I met her. So bright. So beautiful. I know more about her than I ever could through a sync. She wants me to put my hand under her left cheek, with my fingers in her hair, and that's what I do.

I want to kiss her. Can we do that?

She answers by pressing her lips to mine. Her every flash of joy and emotion is known to me, and mine are known to her. We're united.

I don't know how much time passes. A minute, an eternity. It's like swimming in the ocean on a hot summer day—we're tossed about in warmth and love, without any sense of time or place.

Then we want to look out at the light. So we do.

My hand is over hers on the gold railing. Our sides are pressed against each other. We stare at the column of light. It stretches as far as I can see down and up. Around it are other buildings like this one. People dot the balconies, with this same light reflected in their faces. I expected something amazing. I never expected *this*.

"Why are you surprised?" Naomi asks. Her first words.

I think through the possible answers. It all comes back to distant, and flawed, memories from the old earth. I eventually say, "I guess I had a different idea of heaven."

"Like what?"

"I don't know. Something more intangible. I figured we'd be floating spirits, with singing angels all around us. Maybe some harps. I didn't expect to feel your touch like this. I didn't expect to have this body, and to *feel* God's presence. It is so lush, so pristine, so . . . everywhere."

Naomi tilts her head back, with her face basking in the rays that pour over us. "I think He used the sun as an example," she says, "but its light was so much less. It left shadows. It was finite, in a single space, with a determined life. And it burned too hot for us to approach." She breathes in and out deeply. "I love being this close. Just wait until we stand before the throne."

I want that, but I don't want this moment to pass, not yet. I turn to her. "Will we stay together?"

She meets my eyes. "For as long as we desire."

"How long is that?"

She laughs. "For times and times, and then again."

I think of Bart and Evelyn. "Will you live with me here?"

She nods. "And you will live with me. Maybe in time we'll want a journey. We'll travel to the stars."

"I'd like that." I take Naomi's hand in mine, and we walk inside together.

50

MORE TIME PASSES. Naomi and I share a meal. We laugh together. Later we're talking again on the balcony, with the light shining over us, when there's a knock on the door.

"Visitors?" I ask.

"When Jesus brought me here, he said someone would come to take us to the throne." Naomi shrugs. "Don't know who."

"Let's find out." I go to the door and open it.

"Elijah!" My Mom sweeps me into her arms.

We hold each other, half-crying, half-laughing. Eventually she steps back and looks me up and down. "You're the man I knew you could be," she says. "I'm proud of you."

I'm grinning. "Thank you for coming to me, in my dreams."

"Thank the Lord," she says. "He hears the prayers of all—on earth and in heaven. He envisioned your role before he created the earth. All I had to do was my part, trusting in him. We can always trust more than we think."

I'm studying her young face, in awe. I realize she looks about my age. She seems a lot like she did in my old memories of her. I remember that I felt pain at her loss. The pain was dark, broken. But it's gone now—all the pain and the emptiness. There's just the distant idea, a recognition of how things once were and will never be again.

"As I helped you, I too was helped." My Mom steps to the side, and another woman glides into the room.

"Mom!" Naomi rushes past me and embraces the woman.

"We believed you would find each other," the woman says. Her hair and skin are lighter, but she has Naomi's green eyes and freckled nose. "Arella and I sensed it when we first met."

"Elizabeth's right," my Mom adds. "You remember when I was in the hospital?"

I nod, again fascinated by how I can still picture the tubes connected to my Mom, the doctors by her bed, but the memory doesn't hurt anymore.

"That's where we all first met."

"Us?" Naomi is looking at me. I'm as surprised as she is.

"Our rooms were beside each other," my Mom replies. "We discovered we had much in common, including little ones with bright souls."

"You two were God's way of bringing us together," Naomi's mom says.

Our mothers laugh together. "It was amazing," my Mom says. "The first time you met, at the foot of my hospital bed, you just stared into each other's eyes as if the rest of the world had disappeared."

"Really?" Naomi asks. "Wouldn't we remember that?"

"You were only eight," her mom says. "And it was a painful time. We knew that. It's a special grace of God that young minds could block out those pains."

"Yes, and we saw more than just your bond." My Mom gazes at Naomi like she's her own daughter. "We had visions of what was to come. Nothing too clear. Just enough to know that you both had important roles to play. Naomi, your soul was as pure as a young girl's could be. Like Eve's before the fruit, like Mary's." She turns to me. "Elijah, the stain of sin was already heavy on you. I admit that I feared your fate, as I did your father's. I prayed and prayed for him, but some the enemy will hold forever—the vessels of wrath. But not you, praise God. You had the gift of our family. The Roeh, the seers. I knew that, but in those last days on earth, my soul cried out for the darkness to lift from you, so you could use the gift for God's purpose. Oh, a mother's worry knew no bounds!" She sighs and turns to Naomi's mom. "That's why I needed help. That's why God gave me Elizabeth."

"Your mom's faith was immense," Elizabeth says. "Her well was deep and wide, but it wasn't full. She didn't understand the fullness of God's sacrifice, she hadn't learned of Jesus. I just told her what I knew. The Lord did the work from there."

My Mom continues, "As soon as she told me these things, Christ's light flooded into me. I was bubbling over with joy, even as my body suffered. It tore me apart that I couldn't communicate this to you, Elijah. You know how it was those last days. I couldn't speak, and the treatments were as bad as the tumor itself. But, as with all things, the Lord had a purpose. I died in peace."

Elizabeth takes my Mom's hand. "We joined each other in heaven."

"We prayed unceasing for both of you," my Mom says. "Because of your visions, Elijah, and your spirit, the Lord granted that I could come to you a few times in dreams. I couldn't say everything."

I remember her visits: soaring over New York as the flood came, walking the raised path through a swamp, facing the dragon as only a baby in Jerusalem. Those visions helped me understand my weaknesses. They gave me the right kind of fear—the knowledge that I was not the one in control. "You showed enough," I say. "But there are still things I don't understand."

"What would you like to know?"

I turn to Naomi. "Why did God let Don go so far? Why did you have *his* son?"

A smile spreads over Naomi's face. "I thought you

knew! My son is here, perfect as we are. He is with his grandfather now, and he will grow in time. It's like he completed the cycle of humanity on earth. The devil tempted and corrupted the first man in the garden. He wanted to craft a final man full of his spirit. But God saved my son. The first Adam and the last Adam will worship God together."

I remember the baby in the chamber under the Dome—as if filling with the dragon's darkness and evil—but then I remember my own darkness washed white in Christ's light before the throne. "It's still hard to fathom."

"Sin was relentless," Naomi says, "almost as relentless as the Lord's love. Only one could win." She raises her arms into the air, as if to emphasize the weightlessness of this place without sin. "But they had to fight, because we had to choose."

My Mom has been listening to us, watching, and now she says, "I think they're ready."

"For what?" I ask.

"Eternity is not stagnant," Elizabeth says. "We will grow forever closer to the light, forever fuller and richer. And, whenever we wish, we may visit the King. We can bring glory to Him."

My Mom nudges us out the door. "Come on! See for yourself!"

51

THE FOUR OF US go down the elevator and leave the building. Naomi leads us in a song. We walk down a street of gold to the light, and others join us.

I see familiar faces everywhere—angels and humans. Ronaldo, Moses, Zhang Tao and his wife Xi, Tristan and Mara, Neo and little kids from his camp. Even Wade Brown. And so many more. They're all alive. They're walking with us, singing.

Tears of joy fill my eyes. My voice streams forward and channels into the flood of the voices around me. The song lifts us and carries us together to the light. We are the praise. We are one.

We stand before the light now, before God. Nothing separates us. His brilliance leaves no shadow. Every nook and cranny of my being is exposed, and it is wonderful. I feel naked and innocent and wrapped in warmth.

I turn to Naomi. I remember that, once, on earth, her face glowed. This is different. Her face shines with the same light at the center, as if the light has poured into her and now it overflows. We cannot contain this light, yet it courses through our glorified bodies, in and out of me, in and out of her. I wonder at what we look like from a distance, but then I look back at the center. That is what we look like. We are wrapped up in the pillar of light— becoming light. We radiate like candles of the same chandelier, all lit with the same fire, and the fire is God.

"Elijah," says Jesus. His right hand clasps my shoulder. "Naomi," he says, his other hand on her shoulder. He is between us, smiling with such joy that it makes me laugh.

"You see life everlasting as my Father planned? You see the I AM."

I am nodding. I can't answer, can't find the words, but I don't need them. He understands.

I respond by joining the song around me. Naomi does, too. Our voices glorify God. It is like the love and joy of every wedding day combined, and more. Awash in this love, Jesus walks and dances into the pillar of light, where he joins the Father and the Spirit as one. I don't think of what will come next. I am lost in this moment, this eternity—the time that never stops, that I never want to stop, and that never will stop.

THE END

Ω

AUTHOR PAGE

I hope you enjoyed *Great White Throne* and The Omega Trilogy. If so, please share the word and post a review on Amazon. With your help, perhaps this story will bring others to live in revelation. 1 Corinthians 2:10.

If the technology in this book intrigued you, check out the short story, *No God in the Machine*. Read it in a few minutes and you'll never think about machines the same way again. Get your free copy at www.jbsimmons.com/no-god-in-the-machine.

*   *   *

J.B. Simmons lives outside Washington, DC, with his wife and three little kids. He writes before dawn and runs all day. His secret fuel: coffee and leftover juice boxes. To learn about his latest project, visit **www.jbsimmons.com**.

ACKNOWLEDGMENTS

Thanks to Lindsay for making my writing possible, inspiring the big questions, and honing my words. Thanks to my Inklings writer friends, Michael and Danny, for being honest as iron—sharpening my stories and me. Thanks to The Falls Church Anglican for teaching the truth. Thanks to the fantastic beta-readers: Michael, Danny, Anne, Ryan, Jean, Jim, and Laurel. And, finally, thanks to you for reading my work and sharing the word. The journey would not have been complete without you.

OTHER WORKS BY J.B. SIMMONS

Light in the Gloaming
Breaking the Gloaming

In the *Gloaming* books, J.B. Simmons weaves political philosophy into fantasy, like *A Game of Thrones* with a C.S. Lewis twist. The characters champion history's great thinkers, from Machiavelli to Locke to Nietzsche, and bring them to battle, even in the darkest of underground cities: The Gloaming.

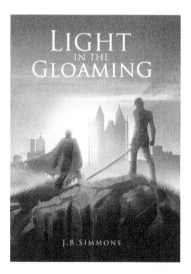

"Tightly crafted . . . a real triumph to creative literature and well deserving of its stars."
Sara Bain, Ivy Moon Press

"A great mix of fantasy, adventure, and allegory." Sunshine Somerville, author, *The Kota Series*

"The characters were outstanding . . . The story was excellent . . . [E]very part of the world is more brilliant in the way the author describes it."
Two Reads Blog

Available on Amazon. Preview at www.jbsimmons.com.

Made in the USA
Monee, IL
30 March 2023